IN TOO DEEP

J. KENNER

IN TOO DEEP

by

J. Kenner

About In Too Deep

Hannah Donovan is not my type.

Intellectual and career-focused, she's a lawyer, and an intimidatingly beautiful one, at that. I'd rather pump iron than open a book, and the only reason I'd go to court would be for a traffic ticket.

She's the most gorgeous woman I've ever seen. So how can I turn down her plea that I pretend to be her fiancé for one weekend?

But I never expected our pretend kisses to feel so real … or for it to lead to a wild night in bed that will forever stand out as the highlight of my sex life.

Our performance convinces everyone, but it was never meant to be more than a fantasy. A short term gig before reality sets back in.

I can't imagine ever being good enough for her, but I'm hooked. And now I'm determined to do whatever it takes to make this fake engagement real.

Meet Mr. October — he's determined to make her his.

Each book in the series is a STANDALONE with NO cliffhanger and a guaranteed HEA!

But even so, you won't want to miss any in the series. Because then you can answer the question...

Who's Your Man of the Month?

Down On Me
Hold On Tight
Need You Now
Start Me Up
Get It On
In Your Eyes
Turn Me On

Shake It Up
All Night Long
In Too Deep
Light My Fire
Walk The Line

and don't miss Bar Bites: A Man of the Month
Cookbook!

Visit manofthemonthbooks.com to learn more!

Chapter One

_____

"WELL?" Easton asked. "What do you think?"

Hannah Donovan turned a slow circle in the sunlit reception area that took up one corner of the seventeenth floor of the Bank of America tower at the corner of Sixth and Congress. Her soon-to-be law partner, Easton Wallace, stood in front of her, a wide grin playing across his classically handsome face. Behind him, Selma Herrington, Easton's girlfriend who had fast become a close friend of Hannah's, stood with her back to them in cut-off shorts and spiky blue hair, her hands pressed to the glass overlooking Austin's famous Sixth Street.

"It's amazing," Hannah said, still having a hard time believing this was real. Were they actually looking at property to lease? For that matter, were they actually opening their own law firm?

She grimaced. Apparently they were. After all, she'd already given notice at Brandywine Consulting where, until yesterday, she'd been gainfully employed as in-house counsel. But as soon as she gave notice, her prick of a boss had suggested that she go ahead and take her accrued vacation. Basically kicking her out the door without even time for cupcakes in the break room.

But that was okay. Because now she was free as a bird. A somewhat terrified bird, facing a brand new adventure.

A bird who didn't have the money she'd counted on to fund this little venture. Because her pig of a former boss had managed to trigger a clause in her retirement plan, leaving Hannah with a retirement nest egg that she was absolutely forbidden to borrow from. And if she closed it out completely and took the money, the penalty was so stiff that she'd barely have enough to buy the whiskey in which to drown her sorrows.

Which meant she was looking at this fabulous office space without her share of the money for their new law firm's start-up capital. Which, of course, included the down payment for this lease.

And that was a fact she hadn't yet shared with Easton.

Now his brow furrowed as he peered at her. "You're way too quiet. Do you not like it?"

Selma turned, her eyes wide. "Of course she likes it. She'd be an idiot not to like it."

"If I didn't, I'd hardly admit it now," Hannah said, amusement overcoming her worries. Selma—in typical Selma fashion—merely shrugged. "And to be clear," Hannah continued, "I do love it. I was—" She cut herself off with a shrug. "I just can't believe it's happening so fast."

That, of course, was the understatement of the year. And she didn't have a clue how to tell Easton that she had to scrape up another source of funds. How horrible to disappoint him that way, especially since she was the one who'd had the original idea for the two of them to form a partnership.

Not only that, but she knew him well, and it was obvious that he'd fallen in love with this space. Hell, she had, too. Just this quick look around and she

3

was convinced that this suite was as perfect for their venture as they'd ever find.

A truly breathtaking space, the suite formed a U that took up half of the east wall, all of the north wall, and the entire west wall. The tiny bit of remaining space was used as storage for the bank that owned the building—which meant that only the employees and clients of Wallace & Donovan, Attorneys At Law, needed to get off at this floor.

A set of double glass doors opened onto the luxurious reception area that faced east and looked out over Sixth Street. But right beside reception was a large conference room—also with glass walls—that faced north and looked down on the historic Driskill Hotel and a tiny hint of the Texas Capitol building. Because of the glass, the room was bright and airy and full of light. But the conference room was designed with automatic blinds, so clients and counsel could work in privacy if necessary.

Offices for associate attorneys—when they hired some—lined the north and west walls, and would also be used for the legal assistants. The northwest corner office boasted a stunning view straight down Congress Avenue, and the southwest corner had a view of the river in the distance. All in all, the space was incredible.

"Nothing wrong with fast when it's right," Easton said to her, though he added a wink to Selma, obviously in honor of their whirlwind romance. "And I really do think it's right. This whole idea is right. This space. Our firm. You and me as partners." He crossed to her and gave her a one-armed hug, the same way he used to congratulate her in law school whenever she got an A or nailed a particularly tricky concept during one of their study sessions. "I've had a good feeling since we took the leap and agreed to do this. Even my crazy notoriety has played into our favor. I'm getting all sorts of calls about folks wanting to talk about representation."

Easton and Selma had been caught with their pants down—or, more specifically, Selma had been caught with her skirt up—not too long ago. The scandal had cost Easton his chance at a judgeship, but as it turned out, he was okay with that. What he really wanted was to practice law—and he'd pulled his name from the race and taken Hannah up on her suggestion that they both quit and open a firm. A suggestion that had been absolutely seaworthy at the time she'd made it, but which had recently begun to spring a few leaks.

"I have a good feeling, too," she assured him. "I swear, I'm not bailing." She wouldn't do that to him. This was too important to them both. This firm was their future. And it represented the kind of law career she wanted. A vibrant practice doing interesting work with a partner she trusted. She'd loved the people at her old job, and she was going to miss seeing her friends everyday. But she'd been about to rot in that environment and had been bored to tears with the actual work.

The in-house job at Brandywine Finance and Consulting had been her second law job. The first had been at a giant law firm where she'd worked for years on cases so huge that she was often only aware of one legal issue—the big picture of the overall litigation wasn't even shared with her.

Some of the work was interesting, but she'd had little client contact, and even less contact with the overall battle plan. She knew she was paying her dues, but after a while she couldn't take it anymore, and she'd accepted the in-house position at Brandywine.

That was better for a while, but after time, the work became rote, and it was no longer about the job but about a steady paycheck. She'd realized almost too late how much she wanted to be out there handling actual cases. Writing detailed briefs that argued real law. Building a practice and making a reputation.

Fortunately, Easton wanted the same thing.

Unfortunately, she'd lost time—most attorneys her age who went out on their own already had a handful of clients in their pocket. Which meant that if she wanted to build the firm up into something successful, she had to put all her focus and energy into this firm. Into making certain that she and Easton succeeded.

"I know you're not bailing," Easton assured her. "But we need to lock this down. If we take too much time, someone will snatch it out from under us. I got first look because the guy who handles leasing for this building owes me a favor. But he'll only hold it open for us to Monday morning. After that, we won't be the only interested parties. Besides, the sooner we commit to this place, the sooner we can start meeting with clients."

Hannah turned in a slow circle, taking it all in. And,

yes, coveting this suite. "This place will definitely wow them." The space had previously housed a defunct law firm, and they had even left their law library behind, a spacious room filled with all the necessary resources, nestled in the interior of the building.

"And you can have your pick of corner offices," Easton said. "Capitol or river view. No drawing straws."

"Really?" She shot a quick glance at her friend.

"Of course you get first dibs. Without you, this wouldn't be happening. "

Her stomach twisted. Because the truth was that even with her it might not be happening. Not unless she could come up with her share of the money.

She drew in a breath and was gathering the courage to tell Easton the hard, cold truth, when Selma threw her hands out to her sides and twirled her way over to Easton in that vivacious Selma way she had. "Well, I love it. But darling, can you afford it?"

"*We*," he said, smiling at Hannah as he brushed his thumb over Selma's lips and pulled her close. "And of course we can. Yes?"

"Absolutely," Hannah said, aiming her smile at both of them and taking a great deal of pride in the fact that her voice didn't crack. Because, dammit, she'd figure out a way. "We'd be crazy not to grab it," she added, as much to convey her enthusiasm as to convince herself. Because it really would be nuts to walk away from such a fabulous deal. Especially when the only tiny stumbling block was Hannah's own lack of funds.

At least the lease had a two-week escape clause, or so Easton had said. Which meant that she had two weeks to either get the money or fess up to Easton.

Surely she could get the money. It wasn't as if she was entirely out of options, after all. There was always her mother and the money that Mom used to call The Hannah Fund. It was out of reach now, true. But maybe, just maybe, she could change that.

She was pondering how to approach her mom— and, more importantly, her stepfather—when she felt the weight of Selma's eyes on her. She glanced up, only to see a glimmer of curiosity cross Selma's face before she turned to Easton and gave him a little shove. "Okay, mister, we're all done here. Go. Do manly things."

His eyes widened, and his lips twitched with obvious amusement. "Trying to get rid of me?"

"Um, duh. Hannah and I have plans," she announced, which was total news to Hannah. "We're off to drink cocktails and ogle hot men. Or women," she added with a glance toward Hannah. "If you'd rather."

Hannah lifted a shoulder, forcing herself not to smile. "Either way, I'm good."

Selma laughed, as Easton cocked one brow. "Just ogling?"

"Don't worry," Selma assured him. "With other men, I only look." She pressed herself against him, her arms going around his waist. "But sometimes that makes the touching later all the more fun. And in case you need it, here's a preview. So you can remember why it's me you come home to." She kissed him—hot and deep and so slow that Hannah was starting to feel like she'd fallen down the rabbit hall into an NC-17 movie.

But when Selma grabbed Easton's ass, it was time to cut the show short. "Okay, you two. Get a room."

As Selma backed away, her expression smug, Easton

held his hands out to his sides and indicated the huge, empty reception area. "A room?" he repeated. "Isn't that why we're here?"

Hannah parked one hand on her hip and cocked her head. "There will be no wild sex on the desks in our law office. Especially since one of us doesn't have anyone to have wild sex with."

On top of everything else, Hannah had been single —and sadly hook-up free—for well over six months now.

Sadly, that state of affairs showed no signs of changing any time soon. A particularly unfortunate fact since an upstanding boyfriend with a good job and decent manners might be the key to solving her current financial crisis.

And, honestly, she missed the fringe benefits, too.

Chapter Two

"OVER SIX MONTHS?" Selma looked so shocked that Hannah almost sank off the stool so she could hide under the long oak bar at The Fix on Sixth. The local Austin bar was not only full of atmosphere, but it also happened to be conveniently located just a few blocks down from what would soon—hopefully, maybe—be Hannah's brand new office.

Coming to the bar had been Selma's idea. Not only did she patronize the place, but Selma's company, Austin Free-Tail Distillery, supplied a variety of whiskeys to the popular bar. Now the women were sitting at a two-top in the smaller back section of the bar, Selma drinking her own whiskey straight-up, and Hannah sipping a Loaded Corona.

"Six months," Selma repeated, studying Hannah's face. "Good God, you're serious."

Hannah felt her ears turn pink. "That's hardly a lifetime."

"Says you."

"I just haven't met anyone I like, and I got tired of doing the hook-up thing, then wasting all that emotional energy wondering if he or she was going to call again."

"I get that," Selma admitted. "But it doesn't explain the weirdness."

Hannah blinked, trying to follow the thread of conversation. "What weirdness?"

"You. In the office. I may not know you as well as Easton does, but I can spot obfuscation a mile away."

"Good God, can you really?" Hannah teased. "Because I can't even spell it."

"Hannah." Selma's voice was flat. Almost parental. "Just spill it, okay? What's going on?"

That was one of the things that Hannah had found so refreshing about Selma the first time they'd met

—the fact that she didn't pull any punches. She said what she meant, and she meant what she said. With Selma, what you saw was what you got.

Usually, that was an amazing trait.

Right now, it was more than a little unnerving.

"Do not even think about dodging the question," Selma said. "Come on. Tell me." She reached out and put her hand over Hannah's, warm and reassuring. "If it's something you don't want Easton to know, I can keep a secret. Or you can talk to someone else. But you need to talk. I see it all over you."

For a moment, Hannah considered telling Selma that she'd find someone else to talk to. But why? Selma was there. Selma would undoubtedly understand.

And most of all, Selma thought outside the box. If anyone would have a creative solution, it would be Selma.

"Right. Well, I'm kind of having a cash flow issue."

Selma leaned back in her chair, nodding slowly. "I thought it might be something like that. What happened?"

Once again, Hannah almost diverted the conversation. After all, talking about money—or at least the lack thereof—ranked way up there on the scale of mortifying topics. But saying nothing wasn't gong to help her. Better to just go for it.

"It's my fault. I thought I'd be able to borrow from my retirement account. You know, for the money that Easton and I are both contributing as operating capital."

"Sure. I'm guessing you can't?"

"Have I mentioned my old boss was a prick?"

Selma laughed. "Once or twice."

"Well, if I'd waited another couple of weeks to quit I would have been fine. But because of the timing—about which I wasn't told in advance—I can't access any of my pension funds. At least not until I actually retire. And I figure Easton doesn't want to wait that long."

"You don't have anything else squirreled away?"

"I did. Then I bought my condo and my car."

"Can you get an equity loan?"

Hannah shook her head. "I got a great deal on my

condo, but the previous owner had trashed it. So I used an equity loan to pay for the repairs and remodel. I told you. I'm screwed. But I don't want to give this up. I mean, I want it. I want the law firm. I want the partnership. And I really don't want to let Easton down." The idea of disappointing her best friend in such a massive way clawed at Hannah's gut. Not only that, but she knew that Easton was relying on their new practice just as she was. Neither of them currently had jobs. This was it. This was their future.

And unless she could figure out a solution, Hannah was going to be the one to make it all go to hell.

"You're going to hate this idea, but Easton's done really well. And not to brag, but Austin Free-Tail is definitely on the rise, too. Either Easton or I could lend you the money. It's not like you're a risky investment."

Hannah shook her head. "Borrowing money from friends means that at the end of the day you have money, but no friends. Not happening."

Selma made a face, but didn't argue. "What other option do you have?"

Hannah sucked in a breath. She had only one other option—and it was a little dicey. Worth it, but dicey.

"What?" Selma prodded. "You're thinking about something. Just spit it out."

"Right. Okay. Here's the thing. This isn't a new idea between Easton and me—the partnership, I mean. I first suggested it years ago, not long after I signed on at Brandywine and realized the work wasn't for me." She rolled her eyes. "I always told everyone I loved it, but the truth was ... well, not so much."

"You're saying you had the money then, but not now. So this was before you bought your condo?"

Hannah shook her head. "No, I already had the condo, and I had my equity loan. But back then, my parents were willing to fund me if I went out on my own."

"*Were* willing," Selma repeated. "But they're not now?"

"Pretty much." She drained the last of her Loaded Corona, then signaled to Eric, the bartender, to make her another. She loved the simple drink—a bottle of Corona with the neck poured off and filled with rum, then topped with a slice of lime—but right now it wasn't about taste. If she was going to talk about her mother and Ernest, she wanted the fortification of a good, old-fashioned buzz.

Across the table, Selma was sitting patiently, but Hannah could see the questions brewing in her eyes. Time to dive in. And why not? Maybe Selma would have a solution.

"Did Easton ever tell you about my dad?"

Selma's brow furrowed; clearly that wasn't the lead-in to the conversation that she'd expected. "I don't think so."

"He died when I was little. Just a toddler, really. He was a cop, and he was killed in the line of duty. It was—well, it was rough. Especially for my mom. Honestly, I don't remember my dad all that well, but my mom really had to scramble. She'd been a housewife, and after he passed, money was really tight. She'd dropped out of school, but she went back, got her degree, and ended up working as a teacher. She was determined to pay my way through college."

"Good for her."

"I know. She was amazing. But money was still tight, and she always told me to be smart. To pick a career where I could make money and always support myself. And she put aside fifty grand of the money from one of my dad's life insurance policies in a savings account. She told me that he'd gotten the policy with me in mind, and she said that she would give the money to me when I was settled with a good job and a solid career, but needed a little extra cash to help me get even farther."

Selma leaned back, her head tilted slightly with obvious confusion.

"Yeah," Hannah said. "I know."

"Then why? Why are we even having this conversation? You're each putting fifty into the business, right? If you have fifty just sitting in the bank…"

Hannah took a second to let the familiar bubble of anger settle. "That would be because of Ernest."

"Who's Ernest?"

"My stepfather. Once he came on the scene, my mom changed her tune. It wasn't the business that mattered, it was my life. She told me that it was still my money, but my father wouldn't have wanted me to fritter my life away working——"

"*Fritter?*"

"That's what she said. And so much more. Bottom line is that I get the money when I'm in a stable relationship. Then, according to my mom, I'll be using it to support my domestic life, even if I decide to put it into my business."

"Wow. Why? Where did that come from?"

Hannah shrugged. She had her theories, but it didn't matter. All that mattered was figuring out a way to get the money.

"So basically, we need to hook you up with someone suitable."

"Who knows? I actually asked for the money about four years ago. I wanted to use it to buy a condo. One that didn't need all the work mine did. And back then, I was in a relationship."

"And she said no?"

"Apparently, she and Ernest didn't like the fact that my partner's name was Janet. But honestly, even if Janet had been a Jack, maybe there would have been some other excuse. I'm probably stupid to think that I'll ever get that money, and it's so frustrating, because I know that Daddy got that second policy so that I'd be taken care of. But he put it in Mom's name, and now I'm screwed."

"Well, you're not with Janet anymore. Maybe your parents could tell it wasn't a permanent thing."

Tiffany, one of the servers, dropped off the fresh Loaded Corona along with a basket of Pretzel Bites with Beer Cheese Dip. "On the house. Eric said you two look like you're doing serious work and needed fuel."

"Serious scheming, you mean," Selma said, with a thank you wave toward Eric.

"Scheming?" Hannah repeated after Tiffany had moved to another table.

"Sure. We just need to find you a relationship. And as for permanence, I'm thinking it only has to be true love until the money's in your hand."

"Yeah, well, I like the way you think." And, honestly, she felt no guilt at all about the possibility of pulling a con on her mom and stepdad. After all, Ernest was practically drowning in money, so it wasn't as if her mom needed the funds. And Hannah's father's wish was for her to have the money. As far as she was concerned, her mom had been playing dirty. And if Hannah had to jump in the mud to get what was hers, then that's what she would do.

Except she needed someone to jump with her, and there wasn't anyone on the horizon. "The problem is that my only option for a potential fake relationship—one that wasn't even really a lie—doesn't work anymore."

"Yeah? Who?"

"Easton."

Selma's eyes went wide and she crossed her arms over her chest. "And it wouldn't be a lie because why?"

Hannah flashed an impish grin. "Because we're partners, right?"

Selma snorted. "True that."

"But seriously, even if I wanted to use Easton as my beard, it wouldn't work. Ernest comes to Austin pretty frequently, and eventually he'd see you and

Easton together. And somehow I don't think he'd appreciate my man cheating on me."

"Probably not. Plan B?"

"If I'm going to do this—and I am, because what choice do I have—I need to have a believable relationship, probably an engagement. I can share the wonderful news this weekend at their annual wedding anniversary party. And then later I can call my mom in tears to tell her about our catastrophic breakup. After the money is in my hands, of course."

"Fair enough. Who?"

She glanced around the bar. Saw a few of her friends who were already paired off as well as several customers she didn't recognize. "I have no idea. Maybe I need to step into the land of fiction. Jean Paul. And he's a French archeologist who teaches at Stanford, but we met when he was doing a seminar in Austin, and now he's on a dig in Africa. But we're madly in love and we're planning a wedding in Provence."

"I thought lawyers were supposed to be better liars."

"Funny. As far as I'm concerned, Jean Paul is the perfect boyfriend."

"Not even close. The secret to lying is sticking close to the truth. Everyone knows that."

"So what are you saying?" Hanna asked.

A wide, slow smile slid across Selma's face. "I'm saying you need to leave it to me."

Chapter Three

"COME ON, GRIFF," Matthew Herrington said as he spotted his newest personal training client. "One more, and you'll hit a personal best."

"Keep goading me, and I'll hit you," Griffin snarled, his arms shaking as he pushed the barbell up higher and higher until Matthew caught it and helped rack the weight.

"That was spectacular," Matthew said, with genuine enthusiasm.

"No kidding." Selma's voice filtered in from across the gym—the *locked* gym—and she started walking over. "How long have you been training, Griff?"

"Not long," Griffin mumbled, his head ducked as

he sat up, then shrugged back into his ever-present hoodie. He zipped the jacket and stood, his back to Selma. "I'm going to go hit the shower. See you around, Selma," he called over his shoulder as he trotted toward the back of the gym.

As soon as he heard the locker room door snap shut, Matthew rounded on his sister. "What the hell is wrong with you?"

"With me? What are you talking about?"

"The man was working out in gym shorts and a tank top. What the hell do you think I'm talking about?"

For a moment, she only looked at him blankly. Then her face cleared, and her eyes widened with horror. "His scars. Oh, shit, Matthew, I'm so sorry. I wasn't thinking. I mean, when I talk to him in The Fix, he's so cool and funny. It didn't even occur to me."

Matthew exhaled noisily, then nodded. How could he stay annoyed with a woman like his sister? Someone who understood why Griff would be self-conscious about his scars, but at the same time really didn't get it at all.

Matthew got it, though. He knew what it was like to have the other kids stare and snicker. Not for his looks—at least, not once he was in high school and started working out—but because of his reading and his grades and his damn stutter. The stutter was long gone, but he was still a slow reader. Still couldn't force himself though the must-read classic novels. And news magazines made his brain come close to exploding.

Math he got. Numbers settled their little asses into their lines and columns and did what they were told. But words…

Well, words could lead him down all sorts of paths, and those paths inevitably ended up twisted around in his mind. And when he was young and had to stand in front of the class, turning beet-red as he tried to wrap his mind and his tongue around the words and the thoughts…

Yeah, he understood why Griffin was self-conscious. Matthew might not have massive burn scars covering half his body, but he knew what it was like to have an unwelcome spotlight shine on you.

"I really am sorry," Selma said, as the silence lingered.

"It'll be okay. But you know, there was a reason I locked the door to the training room." Matthew had a few clients who came in the evenings for personal training appointments, and since the main part of the gym was available 24/7 to any of his gold-level members, Matthew had set up a private training facility in a back room with its own coded entrance.

"I just assumed that you were training."

He almost pointed out that he didn't want to be interrupted while training any more than his clients did, but there came a point with his sister when it was best to just back away slowly. "It'll be fine. Griffin's cool. He knows you didn't mean to embarrass him."

"Do you need to go clear the air with him now?"

Matthew shook his head. "Nah. Chances are he left through the locker room." He sat down on the padded bench that Griff had vacated. "It's past nine, anyway. Why aren't you with Easton? Everything okay?"

"Are you kidding? Everything's perfect. I'm dying for a juice," she added, crossing to the refrigerator in the corner. "I told him I needed to see you. By the way, he said you should come over for dinner soon."

"Sounds like a plan."

There'd been a moment when Matthew had feared that he'd have to beat the living shit out of the lawyer, but Easton had rallied and done himself proud. As far as Matthew could tell, Easton and Selma were about as happy as a couple could get, and Matthew was thrilled that not only was his sister madly in love, but she'd also calmed her wild child ways. At least in public. But so long as Easton could handle her, that was hardly Matthew's concern.

He was, however, a tiny bit jealous, an emotion that was all the more potent since he'd never expected her to settle down—at least not anytime soon. Staying in one place—with one person—had always made her antsy, a fact she'd always blamed on their screwed up childhood. Being abandoned in a mall as a pre-teen by your mother would do that to a person, she'd always said.

To him, though it had done the opposite. He craved stability. A home. A family.

He wanted what his parents had—his *real* parents,

29

not the biological father who'd disappeared or the biological mother who'd left them to fend for themselves in the alcove between Sears and a cookie stand.

For his entire adult life, Matthew had craved a home and a family. And now he was the one living his work, and his ever-wandering sister was the one who'd settled down.

Maybe he shouldn't complain. After all, he had a thriving business and a fat bank account, and that wasn't half-bad for a high school dropout.

But he wanted more. He just wasn't sure how to get it.

"You have that look," she said, returning and handing him a can of coconut water. "Are you still annoyed with me for interrupting?"

"No. It's fine. I was just thinking."

"Yeah? Well, if you're in the mood to think, I'll give you something to noodle over."

"So we're getting down to it?" he asked. "What you needed to see me about?"

"Pretty much," she said, then settled cross-legged

on the floor and looked up to where he was still seated on the bench. "I want you to do a favor for Hannah."

"Hannah?"

She exhaled noisily, buzzing her lips. "Come on, Matthew. You know Hannah. The lawyer. She's even worked out here a couple of times with—oh, with the girl we met at The Fix who's dating Nolan Wood. That drive-time radio guy."

"Shelby," Matthew said. "And of course I know Hannah. I was just surprised that you want me to do a favor for her."

Which was a total lie. He wasn't surprised about the favor. He wasn't even thinking about the favor. All he was thinking of was Hannah. Her bright smile and musical laugh. Those wild blond curls and her slim, strong build. She'd come in a couple of times with Shelby to workout, and watching her do squats in those tight black leggings and the pink workout bra had almost been the death of him.

Hannah Donovan was funny, sexy, and smart as hell. And as far as Matthew knew, she'd never paid him the slightest bit of attention.

"Are you even listening?"

His sister's voice jolted him back from the vivid images of Hannah that had begun to flood his mind.

"What? Yes." He stood, mostly because he simply needed to move. "You said she needs a favor. What kind?"

"I just told you—I knew you weren't listening."

"Selma…"

She lifted a hand in a *never mind* kind of gesture. "She needs you to pretend to be her boyfriend."

He stopped pacing. "What the hell?"

"Honestly, Matthew, you'd really be helping her out."

He sat down again, then bent forward as he dragged his fingers through his hair. When he finally sat up straight again, he wasn't sure if the situation was funny or pathetic. But he'd always prided himself on being an optimistic guy. So he was putting his money on funny. With a splash of pathetic thrown in for good measure. "Listen,

Selma. I know you mean well, but fixing me up this way isn't going to—"

"It's not about you. I swear. And honestly, I kind of misspoke."

"What do you mean?"

"She doesn't need a boyfriend. Or not just any boyfriend. She needs a serious guy. Like, honestly, a fiancé would be perfect."

He gaped at her. "Are you crazy?"

"A little. Why? Is that a problem? It would all just be pretend."

He pushed back onto his feet and started pacing. "I swear to God, Selma, I love you to death. But either I'm one hell of a lot slower on the uptake than I like to believe, or you are intentionally messing with me."

"I'm not. I swear. It's just—oh, hell. It's complicated."

"Then simplify it."

She blew out a breath. "Fine. Selma's dad wanted her to have fifty grand in life insurance money. But Selma's mom has control of the money and she's not forking it over until Hannah is all set up in the throes of domestic bliss. There." She lifted a shoulder. "Guess that wasn't so complicated after all."

"Complicated? I think you skipped over complicated and moved straight to insane. Not hard to explain, but pretty damn impossible to pull off."

"Oh, come on," she urged. "You could totally manage it."

He stared her down. "And you're in the middle of this because?"

"Well, duh. Because of Easton."

He made a whooshing motion over his head. "Can we try that one again?"

She rolled her eyes, looking more like the little sister of their youth than she had in years. "She's Easton's best friend. They're planning to open a law firm together. But she's strapped for cash, and she's not comfortable letting Easton finance the whole venture."

"And if she doesn't get her inheritance, then she may pull out of the partnership with Easton," he filled in.

"Which would completely suck for everybody," she finished for him. "I knew you'd get it. So you'll help?"

"Selma…"

"Please? As a favor to me? Your wonderful sister who loves you? It's important to Easton. After everything that happened after that fiasco at the Children's Museum—"

His eyes widened. "You're laying that at my feet? I wasn't the one photographed with my skirt up around my ears."

"It wasn't *that* high. And we were behind closed doors. It's not our fault if no one knows how to knock these days. The point is," she rushed on, "that getting this law firm off the ground is impor- tant to Easton. And it's important to Hannah, too. And I've seen the way you look at her. This won't exactly be torture for you."

"I'd have to be dead not to look at her, but she's not my type." That was a total lie. But it was close enough, since he was damn sure that *he* wasn't *her* type. "And on top of that, I seriously doubt that I'm the guy who's going to make her parents leap for joy."

"You're a man. Trust me. With Hannah's family, that's plenty to make them happy." She looked at him with wide, puppy dog eyes. "Will you do it?"

As far as Matthew was concerned, the whole thing sounded like a recipe for disaster. But instead of saying no, he waffled. "I'll think about it."

Selma's smile bloomed wider than it should for such a vague response, and Matthew was left with the sinking feeling that he hadn't heard the last of this. "Thanks, big brother. I can't ask for more than that."

Chapter Four

"I GOT IT!" Elena Anderson practically sprinted across The Fix toward the table where Hannah and Selma were sharing a Friday evening pitcher of The Fix's amazing Pinot Punch and chowing down on Pimento Cheese Poppers. "You are looking at the newest employee of the Austin Center for Downtown Conservation and Revitalization."

The daughter of The Fix's owner, Tyree, Elena had short hair, beautifully sculpted cheekbones, and skin as dark as her father's. At the moment, she also had the widest smile that Hannah had ever seen.

Hannah didn't know Elena well, but even so, she jumped up and followed Selma's lead in giving the other woman a quick hug and heartfelt congratulations.

"Thanks so much," Elena said when they were seated again. She filled one of the empty glasses with punch and raised it. "To the start of my fabulous career," she said, and they all clinked glasses.

"Elena wants to go into urban planning—she's starting a graduate program in the fall," Selma explained.

"I'm hoping to specialize in the planning of growing communities, especially towns with a lot of history—like Georgetown," Elena said, referring to a small town about thirty miles north of Austin. "Regulating and planning growth while maintaining the character of towns with an historic Main Street or a square. That's what really interests me. And that's what the ACDCR is all about."

"That sounds really fascinating," Hannah said.

"Ultimately, I want to work for a statewide or national consulting firm, but this is a great beginning, and considering all the talk about historic preservation along Sixth Street, it's going to be terrific experience."

Selma reached over and grabbed Elena's hand. "I'm so excited for you."

"Yeah, well I owe you big time, you know."

"Really?" Hannah asked. "Why?"

Selma lifted a shoulder in a casual shrug. "I didn't do anything but say that Elena's awesome."

"Yeah, well Ms. Gonzales really likes you. She talked about what an excellent job you did restoring the building that houses the distillery, and how much she appreciates it when you donate stock to benefits, and on and on and on."

"Like I said, all I did was sing your praises."

"Well, I appreciate it," Elena added. "Of course, I think she's also impressed that my dad owns this building. It has quite a history, too, you know. But at the end of the day, I'm giving you credit for helping me land the job. And in your honor, I'll buy the next round."

"In that case, I will happily accept the credit," Selma said, then turned to Hannah. "See? I got her a job and you a fiancé. Honestly, I think I earned major friendship points this week."

"Wait. What?" Hannah leaned forward. "Have I been drinking too much punch or did you say that you found me a man."

Selma sat back, buffing her nails against her chest. "Am I good, or what?"

"You're amazing. But who?"

"Matthew, of course."

"Seriously?" Elena's eyes were wide. "He agreed to pretend to be engaged to Hannah?"

"She told you about that?" Hannah asked Elena, who had the grace to look sheepish. "I mean, it's okay. It's not a secret. Well, except to my parents."

"I only told Elena that I'd asked him," Selma clarified, frowning at Elena. "And of course he's happy to do it. He's completely down with the whole idea."

"Really?" Hannah couldn't keep the dubious note out of her voice. "That doesn't seem like him at all."

"Oh, please," Selma countered. "He's quiet and a little shy, but he's always down for helping a friend."

"I guess so. I mean he—*oh.*" There he was, the man

in question, coming out of the small back bar with Landon Ware, a local detective who was dating Taylor, another employee at The Fix.

Boyfriend. The word filled Hannah's mind, and she swallowed. Matthew could definitely fill that role to her satisfaction. He was too good-looking by half with that perfectly cut body, his broad shoulders, and angled face accentuated by an aquiline nose that gave him a sophisticated cowboy kind of look. It wasn't just his appearance that was attractive, either. He had a quiet, easy-going way about him that seemed very Texas-like, as if he was used to spending long days alone on a ranch. And wasn't there a song about a lover with slow hands and—

Yeah. Better not go there.

She stood up. "I should go tell him how much I appreciate him doing this."

"Oh, don't do that now," Selma said. "If you talk to him now, he'll just have to explain to Landon."

"True. I guess I can—oh, he's free. Be right back." She heard Selma call after her as she hurried toward Matthew, but she couldn't hear her friend over the din. She kept on going, determined to tell her newfound savior how thankful she was that he'd do such a huge favor for a woman who was practically a stranger.

She'd crossed half the bar when she saw that Megan Clark had reached him first. A cold knot that had to be frustration—it could hardly be jealousy—settled in her stomach, and she willed it away, then casually continued on toward the bar. She ended up taking an empty stool a few seats behind Matthew. She ordered a shot of Selma's Bat Bourbon, then shamelessly eavesdropped as Megan asked Matthew to please reconsider.

"It's good for business, after all," she said. "Nolan told me his stats are up since he won Mr. April, and he's getting even more callers during his show."

"Megan…"

"And that whole scandal with Easton and Selma? Totally kicked off the radar after he won the Man of the Month contest."

That was not only true, but Megan's words also clued her in to the topic—apparently Megan was trying to convince Matthew to enter the Man of the Month contest, a bi-weekly calendar guy contest that the folks at The Fix had started as a way to get more attention for the bar, which had been in some financial trouble at the time. As far as Hannah knew, it had worked, because the place always seemed crowded and solvent.

Hannah hoped the bar wasn't in danger of closing, because she loved the place. It felt like home, with the familiar faces and the mouthwatering menu. Plus, she really wanted to see Matthew in that contest, and she had a feeling that might be a long time coming. She'd heard through the grapevine that he'd already turned Megan down multiple times.

"Please," Megan added. "You'll end up on Brooke and Spencer's reality show, too. And think of all the possible new clients you might woo."

Matthew chuckled, the sound low and enticing even where Hannah was sitting. "Did you actually say 'woo'?"

"I'll say whatever you want if you just tell me the magic words."

"Okay."

"Well?" Megan pressed.

Matthew chuckled. "I said okay."

"I know. Just tell me what you want me to say and I'll—*oh*. You mean you'll do it? You'll actually enter the Mr. October contest?"

"You wore me down. Or maybe your wooing did."

"You are the best," she said. "I have to go tell Jenna," she added, referring to one of the co-owners of the bar with Tyree. "Seriously, thank you so much."

As Megan practically bounced toward the hallway that led to the kitchen and office space, Hannah slipped off her stool and walked around to face Matthew. "Hey," she said, then immediately apologized when he choked on his drink.

"Hannah. Sorry." He coughed and took a deep breath. "Didn't see you there."

"I didn't mean to scare you. I just wanted to thank you for agreeing to join me in this farce."

He cocked his head, his brow furrowed.

"Our fake relationship, I mean." She nodded toward Selma, who responded with a listless three-finger wave.

"Oh. Right. Sorry," he said with a small frown. "I had to shift gears there for a minute."

"Selma told me you'd come on board. Surprised the hell out of me, but then I overheard you just now with Megan…" She trailed off with a shrug. "Guess you're doing favors for all the girls."

For a moment, he simply looked at Selma. Then he chuckled and said, "Yeah. I'm probably crazy for doing it, but it's not like I can turn either of you away."

"You're a lifesaver," she said. "And doing this so last minute is particularly spectacular of you." And then, without thinking about it, she put her hand on his shoulder, leaned forward, and brushed a quick kiss over his cheek. He smelled like a forest after a rainstorm, fresh and clean, and she lingered a moment, thinking that there was something comforting about the scent of him and the strength she felt beneath her palm.

Maybe this was a stupid thing that she was doing, but in that moment at least, she was glad it was Matthew who was going into the fray with her. Because if nothing else, she was certain that he'd hold her close, play the part, and catch her if she stumbled.

She pulled away, feeling gooey and a little shy as she smiled weakly at him. "Anyway, thanks. I'll load you up on all the info about everyone during the drive tomorrow. Three hours to Dallas should be plenty of time for us to make up and memorize our story. So I'll come get you at nine, okay?"

Chapter Five

MATTHEW WAS AWAKE BY FIVE. By seven-fifteen, he'd gotten in a two-hour workout, including a three-mile run along the river.

By eight he'd finished breakfast, and by nine he'd run out of things to do except worry.

Which pretty much put him back where he'd started, as he'd been worrying—or, more accurately, he'd been kicking himself—since Hannah cornered him in the bar last night.

Not that the actual cornering had been unpleasant.

On the contrary, the sensation of being near her had been spectacular. He'd felt it—felt *her*—humming through him. Like he'd walked too close to a transformer, and his body had begun to buzz from the electricity in the air. He'd wanted to touch her simply to find out if sparks would shoot from his fingers. And when her lips had brushed his cheeks, it had taken all of his effort not to turn his head and taste that sweet mouth.

She'd made an impression, all right. She'd fired his senses. Struck a nerve.

Whatever you wanted to call it, she'd done it.

Which probably explained why he'd agreed to participate in this scheme. More, it probably explained why he hadn't politely but firmly backed away when she'd texted him last night.

He'd read it so many times he could practically recite it: *Hey, it's Hannah. You looked a little bit spooked in the bar, and I started to wonder if maybe Selma hadn't completely filled you in. The party's tomorrow at my parents' house in Dallas. Drive up Saturday, come back Sunday. I thought Selma had told you, but knowing Selma...*

Anyway. Hope that's still okay. Ping me back if you need to bail. I'll understand. XOXO, Hannah.

She'd signed it with hugs and kisses.

How could he bail after that?

He couldn't, of course. Which was why he'd written back a quick text that completely absolved his sister, said that he was looking forward to the drive, and promised to download a couple of playlists for the road.

At the time, he'd thought of it as an adventure. He was a chivalrous guy doing a woman a favor.

Now, he'd amended *chivalrous* to *foolish.* Because honestly, how could this possibly end well?

He was still pondering that when the doorbell rang and he almost jumped out of his skin.

Also foolish. Because this wasn't a date. He had nothing at all riding on it. Nothing at all to be nervous about.

Nothing, that is, except the fear that he'd slide deeper and deeper in lust with her. That he'd realize she was funnier than he'd first thought, prettier than he'd seen. He'd want more—

And he'd be denied.

And that, he thought, seemed to be the story of his life.

"Get a grip, Herrington," he muttered to himself as

he headed to the door. "This isn't a first date. You're not logged into some dating app trying to find true love. She's not looking for anything more than cash, and you're her ticket to payday."

Good advice.

All he had to do was remember it—and try not to screw it all up for her.

With one final, fortifying breath, he pulled open the door and felt his stomach slip to his knees. *God, she was gorgeous.*

Her blond curls bounced in the September sunlight, streaks of copper giving credence to his memory of the sparks that seemed to have arced between them. She wore a maxi skirt that clung to her hips and accentuated her thighs, along with a pale pink V-neck blouse that managed to look both casual and classy. She wore minimal makeup, but her lips were lush and red and so very kissable.

"You look fabulous," he said as she stepped inside, and damned if his voice didn't break like a teenager's.

"Thanks. So do you."

"I wasn't sure about the dress code." He was

wearing jeans, a plain white tee, and a pale blue button down shirt.

"You look perfect. Very Texas. And if my parents are true to form, this will be a cocktail party on the ground floor, with the doors to the patio wide open. An indoor-outdoor thing with lots of alcohol and limitless barbecue."

"Well, at least that part won't suck."

She laughed. "So you're expecting the rest of it to be a nightmare?"

"I'm just hoping I don't screw it up for you."

Her sweet smile shot straight to his heart. "You couldn't possibly." She nodded to the leather duffel he was using as an overnight bag. "If you're ready, we should probably hit the road."

He bent to pick up the bag. "Yeah," he said. "I'm as ready as I'll ever be."

NERVOUS WASN'T EXACTLY the right word, but Hannah had definitely been feeling some trepidation before she and Matthew started out on their two hundred-mile journey from Austin to Dallas. Highland Park, actually. An upscale community surrounded by the city of Dallas.

By all rights, she should have been nervous about the upcoming party. Ernest wasn't a fool, and neither was her mother. If they knew that she was putting on a show just to get the money...

But what choice did she have? And besides, it was too late now. She'd made her plan; now she just needed to follow it.

That, however, wasn't what had set her nerves to humming before they'd hit the road. Instead, she was all too aware of the man who would be joining her. A man who—for no reason other than loyalty to his sister and the kindness of his heart—was doing this awesome favor for her. Maybe she was making more out of it than she should, but the whole thing seemed so sweet. So chivalrous. Like she was a lost princess and he was a knight in shining armor.

All of which was why she'd expected the trip to be mostly quiet and a little awkward, with the two of them being overly polite in order to compensate for her ridiculous case of nerves.

Instead, he'd plugged in his phone, hit a button, and within minutes they were jamming to a playlist full of everything from Michael Jackson to Ed Sheeran to P!nk. Then, after a dozen or so tracks, he'd turned down the volume, and they'd slid seamlessly into a conversation about their first concert experience.

"I was twelve," he told her, "and still getting used to having a real family. Don't get me wrong, I adored the Herringtons, but they weren't even officially our parents yet. We were still fostering. And then one day they said they were taking us to a concert. They took us to see Eminem—because someone had told them that was who all the kids loved."

"But you didn't." Laughter filled her voice as she tried to picture him politely telling his new parents that he'd love to go.

"Not me. Not even Selma. But we both pretended like we did. We faked singing along. We screamed when he came on stage. We ended up competing against each other to see who could fake being a bigger fan. And in the end, we had one of the best nights we'd ever had."

"Did you tell them?" She took her eyes off the road only long enough to see his face.

"Not even to this day."

"They sound really great."

"Yeah," he agreed. "They are. We drew the short straw at birth, but we got lucky in the end. What about you?"

"I was a toddler when my dad died, so no concerts with him for me."

"I'm sorry."

"Thanks," she said, because what else was there to say?

"I know your mom struggled after that, but she obviously held onto the life insurance money that your dad had earmarked for you. She still has it, after all."

Hannah tightened her grip on the steering wheel. "Yeah. She's still got it."

"If she's not using it, and if your father wanted you to have it, why doesn't she just give it to you? Was it your dad's wish that you be in a relationship?"

"No," Hannah said sharply, then shook her head. "If that's what Daddy had wanted, then I wouldn't take the money until I was fully committed to someone. All he said was that it was for me."

"Then why?"

"Because my mother…oh, hell. It's like she found Ernest, and everything she used to think or believe went flying out the window."

"Ernest is your stepfather."

He spoke the words as a statement, but she nodded anyway. "They got married long after Mom had put herself through school and started working as a teacher. But he changed the dynamic completely. I was about to start law school, so I wasn't around much, but we get along okay. About most things."

"What does he do? He's a lawyer, too, right?"

"What doesn't he do? He's a lawyer, but he doesn't practice so much as he consults and lobbies. He owns a couple of companies and sits on about a dozen boards. As far as my mom is concerned, the two of them are the picture of all that is right and good in the world of marital bliss." She grimaced.

"I don't know. Maybe they really are happy. But the way she talks about my dad now…"

"How?"

Hannah blinked. No way was she going to cry while she was driving. "Like she'll say that he never should have been a cop—he was killed in the line of duty. She says he put his family at risk by putting himself at risk. And she never talks about what a hero he was anymore. He died saving a woman who'd been held hostage by a drug dealer. That used to make her so proud. Now she says it's a waste. And every time she says it, I can imagine her mentally sorting through all of her various bank and brokerage account statements. Because she and Ernest have told me more than once that he was such a talented man to have wasted it all on such a base occupation. Not even profession. They can't even grant him that. *Shit*," she added, then wiped away the tear that was tickling the tip of her nose.

"I'm so sorry."

Hannah shrugged. "Yeah. Me, too." She sniffled. "I blame Ernest, but all of that must have been in my mom somewhere, you know? And even though she says that she loved my dad with all her heart and always will, she still completely discounts what he did. Guess it's a good thing I went to law school, right? Otherwise she'd probably completely disown me."

She sniffed, then forced a smile. "And speak of the devil," she said brightly, more to change the subject than for any other reason. "We're in Waco. This is where I went to school. Baylor Law, right over there."

She pointed vaguely to her right, indicating the entire Baylor campus.

"Did you like it?"

"What? Law school? I loved it. Not the mock trial stuff—Easton's the showman who thinks on his feet —but I loved the research and the analysis and the legal arguments. I mean, Constitutional Law? I jammed on that class." She glanced at him. "That's one of the things that I disliked about my old job. I was in-house counsel. Everything was paper-push-ing. Very little thinking. Very little that felt like I was stretching myself. You know?"

"Honestly, no. Academics really aren't my thing."

"But you still get it. I've seen you at the gym. The

way you push your clients. And you've opened other branches. That's stretching. Doing. You're not just going through the motions."

She glanced sideways at him. "Right?"

"Maybe. But——"

An electronic ringtone interrupted them, the display revealing that the caller was Hannah's mother. With a sigh, she pressed the button to accept the call.

"Hey, Mom."

"Sweetie, so good to hear your voice. I just wanted to make sure I understood you. The young man you're dating will be joining you this evening?"

"Absolutely."

"Oh, good. Is he with you?"

"Right beside me," Hannah said. "But he's got his headphones in, and he's asleep. So you'll have to wait to grill him about his intentions until you meet him."

"Funny girl. I'm not going to grill him or embarrass you."

"I'll believe it when I see it."

"My daughter the smart ass."

Hannah grinned. "I take after my dad."

"Speaking of your father," her mother said, and Hannah bristled, "Ernest and I are dying to know more about this young man. You said his name was Matthew? What does he do?"

She changed lanes, and when she glanced over toward the man in question, she saw that he was fighting a smile. "Business," she said with an apologetic shrug. "He owns his own business."

"That's wonderful. What type of business?"

"He's in health."

Matthew's brows rose, and she mouthed, *Well, it's true.*

"A doctor?"

"No."

"No?" Her mother's voice practically dripped with disappointment.

Matthew leaned over and hit the mute button on the console. "Tell her I dropped out of med school.

That I realized I was too entrepreneurial to play it safe being a doctor."

She lifted a brow in question, and when he nodded, she shrugged. If he was getting into the spirit, then she sure as hell wasn't going to argue.

"Not a doctor," she said after unmuting the call. "But that's because he left med school to go to business school."

"Is that so? Well, he sounds like exactly the kind of man your father wanted for you."

Hannah clutched the steering wheel tighter but didn't comment, even though she knew damn well that her father only wanted her to be happy. Ernest was the one with the revisionist memory.

"We'll see you when you get here. Drive safe."

"We will," she promised before wrapping the conversation and then exhaling loudly. "Thanks for that," she said. "Definitely easier to pull off a conspiracy if my co-conspirator's on the same page."

"Who knows? If I keep getting deep into character, I may run an entire pharmaceutical company by the time we actually get to Dallas."

"Yeah, well we're not even in Hillsboro yet. We still have about two hours to go, and we've already converted you from a gym owner to a med student to an MBA."

"We just said business school," he protested.

"Trust me. By the time we hit Dallas expectations will be high." She let her eyes rake over him again, remembering the way he'd filled out the jeans as he'd carried his duffel to the car. He looked hot, no doubt about that. But did he look like a business mogul who worked in healthcare?

"What?" he asked, warily.

"It's just—don't get me wrong, you look great. But—"

"I'm not the guy we just invented."

"Sorry."

He ran his fingers through his hair. "We'll pass North Park Mall before we hit your mom's place."

"Maybe we should stop and do a little shopping?"

"Probably should," he said. "After all, your parents want a certain kind of guy, right? A different kind of guy."

"Maybe they do," she said. "But I want you." She did, too. Who else would go through all this for her? The guy was like a miracle who'd walked into her life.

"You mean you need me."

"Well, yeah," she said. "That, too."

Chapter Six

THIS, Matthew thought as he looked around the huge house nestled in the middle of one of the metroplex's most prestigious neighborhood, *was not what he'd expected.*

He knew that Hannah's stepfather was a prominent attorney-turned-businessman—much like the role Matthew was playing—but considering that Hannah had told him on the drive about how her mother had scraped together pennies to get an education and raise Hannah, he'd expected a much more modest home.

This place was a mansion. A huge mansion. On a massive yard. A multimillion-dollar oasis in the middle of urban sprawl. He'd been uncertain about stopping at the mall for new clothes. Now he was relieved they had. He had a feeling he was going to fit in better with the blue blazer, khaki slacks, and pale gray knit shirt he now wore.

"You ready?" Hannah asked as she steered the car in front of a valet, then shifted into park.

"I hope so," he said. He wanted to ask her what kind of mother denied her daughter life insurance proceeds when she obviously didn't need the money, but why ask rhetorical questions?

He hated the fact that Hannah had to come crawling back, but seeing the house made him all the more determined to play his role perfectly. Whatever it took, Hannah should have her money.

"The reception is on the back patio, through the main hall," the valet told her.

"Thanks, I know. This is my mother's house. Could you ask Clarence to see about the bags in the trunk? We're staying overnight."

"Of course. And welcome home."

He saw her smirk, but she didn't comment. He knew she didn't consider this luxurious property her home, so he said nothing either. Not about that. He did ask who Clarence was.

"The butler," she said. "A nice guy, though I don't know him well. Obviously all of this—" She waved to encompass the entire property, "—came after I'd moved away from Mom."

"Butler," he said. "I didn't realize when I said I'd come with you that we'd be dining at a castle."

"Yeah, well, I like to plan spectacular first dates." She flashed him a teasing grin, but his mind was locked on that one word—*date*. This wasn't a date, and he needed to remember that. But the truth was, he liked Hannah, and if he wasn't careful, he might find himself in too deep. Because he knew damn well that this wasn't about them. This was about her work. Her ambition. And he really wasn't a part of that.

They crossed a granite plaza that led to the front door—a huge glass and iron entryway that stood wide open at the moment, giving them a view of the marble-floored entrance hall that was lined with various cocktail stations. One for martinis, one for wine, one for Scotch and whiskey. He noticed a few of Selma's labels on the whiskey table and resisted the urge to pull out his cell phone and take a picture.

"Wow. This is…"

"Ostentatious?" she supplied. "Yeah, Ernest isn't one for subtle. But the nice thing is that it's easier to blend in. If we were just coming to meet the parents, you'd be on stage every second."

She made a good point.

"Hungry?"

"I could eat." If nothing else, it would give him time to get settled. After his early years of nomadic poverty, he'd grown up comfortably in a well-to-do Austin neighborhood. But the Herrington family home was a pup tent compared to this place.

"Then come on. If history is any indication, Mom catered every food imaginable. Personally, I'm a hot dog and barbecue kind of girl. And even though she always has tons of frou-frou food, she never skimps on the brisket and link sausages."

"Lead the way," he said, startled when she slid her hand into his. His surprise must have shown, because she offered him a sweet smile. "We're engaged, right?"

He nodded, hoping he looked casual. But the truth was that her fingers twined with his felt a little too good. Too *right*.

Which was ridiculous, because if he was thinking along those lines, he was all wrong.

They'd just stepped from the ornate entrance hall through the open French doors and onto the flagstone patio when a slender woman in her late fifties hurried up to them. She wore a white gown, and her hair—the same color as Hannah's—was piled on her head and partially concealed under her veil.

And her smile when she saw her daughter rivaled the sun.

"The blushing bride," Hannah said, then turned to Matthew. "I forgot to tell you. Mom and Ernest repeat their vows to each other every year. They do that in private, but then this party is essentially a wedding reception. And we're here to celebrate the bride and the groom."

"That's lovely," he said, meaning it. He wasn't sure he'd want an annual party, but a private vow renewal on a wedding anniversary was the kind of tradition he could get behind.

"Maybe the two of you can adopt our tradition," Hannah's mother said before turning to her daughter. "Sugar, I'm so glad you're here."

She pulled Hannah into a monster of a hug, her affection for her daughter so obvious it shocked Matthew. Considering the money she was withholding, he'd been expecting a cold, calculating woman. And now he had to hold in his surprise as he watched Hannah return her mom's embrace with obvious enthusiasm.

When they broke apart, Hannah reached out her hand for his, and the simple gesture tugged at his heart. That sense of being a team. Of having a partner in the world. Someone you loved and who loved you back.

For this weekend, apparently, it was his to enjoy.

Too bad it was all fake.

"Mom, I want you to meet Matthew Herrington. My boyfriend. And," she added as she squeezed his hand, "my fiancé."

"You're engaged! Oh, darling that's wonderful." She swooped Hannah into a hug, causing her to release his hand. Then she turned back to him and clutched his hands in hers. "I'm so thrilled. And thank you so much for coming to our celebration. I'm all flustered. And please call me Amelia. Or Mom."

"It's a pleasure, Amelia," he said, then caught Hannah's eye as she squeezed his fingers. He stepped closer, releasing her long enough to slide his arm around her. Without hesitating, she leaned against him, the scent of her shampoo as intoxicating as the whiskey he needed if he was going to get through this day without going completely insane.

"Hannah's been so busy I haven't had the chance to get all the details about you from her."

"And there's no time now, Mom. You've got over a hundred guests wandering around. Don't you have to go play hostess?"

From what Matthew could see, a hundred was probably an understatement. The back yard was huge—probably two acres of well-manicured land with a pool, tennis courts, and a cabana. Not to mention the massive patio on which they were standing. And everywhere he looked, people were mingling.

"When you told me it was a backyard barbecue, this really wasn't what I had in mind," he told Hannah after Amelia had wandered off.

"Wishful thinking," she said. "When I was growing up, Mom and I used to grab barbecue from this local dive, then take it back to the duplex we rented and have a party on the back porch. If it was summer, we'd lounge in one of those blow-up pools, too. We didn't have money for anything else. My aunt kept telling Mom she should just go on welfare, but that wasn't an option. She worked her but off, saved, and made it." Again, she flashed a smile. "And some of my best memories are things I wouldn't have had if we'd had money. Like the blow-up pool picnics."

"This was when you were really little, then?"

She laughed. "Nope. Probably sixteen. I used to love that stupid pool. I think I read every novel ever written while sprawled across one, my butt in the water and my head resting on the plastic. So awesome." She sighed. "Guess Mom's got it better now, though."

He squeezed her hand. "She seems happy. And from what I see she really loves you. I don't know why she's holding back the money your dad left for you, but I don't think it's out of spite."

"I don't either. It's—never mind." She started to turn away, but he took her elbow.

"What?"

"It seems like she lost herself when she married Ernest. Like with my dad—and with his memory—she was the person she really is. But with Ernest, she's playing a part. And I think...I don't know... sometimes I think that's the danger of a relationship. You end up losing yourself because you try to squeeze into a mold."

"Is that why you're not in a relationship?"

"Maybe. I don't know. Probably."

"Well, for what it's worth, I think you're wrong. Honestly, I believe it's just the opposite. A good relationship can help you be the person you really are."

Her mouth quirked as she considered the words. "Maybe. I don't know. I guess I haven't had a really good relationship—not romantically or professionally."

"Meaning?" A waiter came by offering margaritas,

and he grabbed two, then led her to a small stone bench at the edge of the patio.

"Obvious, don't you think? I've never found someone I can completely be myself with."

"Huh," he said. "Have you been looking?"

She laughed. "Not really. And I don't intend to start. Not now when I'm diving into building a business. That's a terrible time to try to have a relationship."

Matthew had to agree. In fact, he was going the opposite direction. After spending more hours than he liked to think about working on his business, he was seriously considering cutting back. Because he wanted the family. A woman he loved. Kids. Maybe a dog. And it was too damn hard finding someone while he was wrapped up in work. And even if he did find her, how the hell could he build a family if he was bouncing between locations and setting up franchises?

"What?" he said, realizing his rambling thoughts had overlapped something she'd said.

"All I said was that I'm sticking with friends. Romance can wait."

"Because you can be yourself with friends."

Her smile was like an arrow to his heart. "I'm being myself with you, aren't I? Even though to the rest of the world it's an act."

"Method acting?" he said, then immediately regretted it. But she didn't seem to mind. Instead, she took his hand, then lifted it to her lips. He shivered as she brushed a kiss over his knuckles, then leaned sideways so that her mouth was just millimeters from his ear.

"Pretend I'm saying something ridiculously naughty and X-rated," she said. "My mom's watching, and my dad is beside her."

"Your dad?" he murmured, while he reached over and cupped his hand on her thigh over her skirt. She inched closer, and he slid his hand up just a bit higher, all the while thinking that it was a good thing the skirt was long, because since they were method acting, he would have happily pulled up the material of a shorter skirt just to feel her skin burn beneath his hand.

"They didn't get married until I was in law school, but he likes me to call him Dad when I'm home." She shrugged. "I didn't at first, but it made things uncomfortable between him and my mom, so I gave up the battle and tried to make it a habit. I figure it's a small price for peace."

"Wise."

"I guess." She'd been toying with his hand as they whispered, and now she released him. "They've moved on. We can quit the young lovers routine."

"Do we have to?" The moment the words were out of his mouth, he wanted to call them back. The comment had just come out—heartfelt, maybe, but not something he would have said to her if he'd been thinking.

But he hadn't been thinking, because this woman tended to steal all his thoughts away.

"I didn't—"

"We don't have to stop," she said softly, turning her face just enough so that he could see her eyes. "Method acting, remember."

"Right." He swallowed, and maybe it was his imagination, but he thought she leaned just a bit closer. Her lips parting for a kiss. And all he had to do was—

"Oh. My. God. Hannah! Look at you! I haven't seen you since last year!"

"Aunt Beatrice! So great to see you." She stood and gave the sixty-something woman a hug, then introduced her to Matthew, who'd been trying to decide if she was as disappointed as he was that their almost-kiss had been interrupted.

"A pleasure to meet you," he said, standing and trying to recall his manners.

"Beatrice is my mom's older sister."

"And I need to steal you away, dear. Amelia says you two are engaged and I want to hear everything. But I want all the dish," she added with a wink. "That means you're not invited, young man. But surely you can live without her for a few minutes."

"I don't know that I can," he said, playing the role.

But as she walked away with her aunt, he couldn't help but think that there might have been a bit of truth in those words after all.

MATTHEW WAS FILLING his plate with sliced brisket

and potato salad when Hannah returned, her mere proximity sending awareness coursing through him. She pressed her palm against his back, then leaned close, her manner so casual it almost seemed as if they really were dating. But, hey, method acting, right?

Then again, maybe she was just good at deception. Usually, Matthew wasn't. But in this case it wasn't difficult to appear head-over-heels for his pretend fiancée, because Hannah Donovan had mesmerized him from the first moment he'd met her.

"Hey, stud," she said. "If you get the food, I'll grab some wine. I got us a table near the band. And after the bride and groom do the first dance, we can go out on the floor, too. Less talking to people about our engagement if we're lost in each other's arms, right?"

He swallowed, imagining the feel of her against him during a slow dance. "Sounds good. I'll meet you at the table in a—"

"Oh, *hell*. Red alert." The harsh, almost scared, tone of her voice cut through him, making him want to hold her close and soothe her. "It's my dad. Ernest."

His stomach curdled, his protective instincts now warring with a strong urge to just get the hell out of there.

But he couldn't. The man was the entire reason he and Hannah were at this wedding together. Why they were pretending to be engaged. Why she'd been looking at him all gooey-eyed for most of the evening, and he'd been diligently reminding himself that it was fake. All fake.

"Let's head over and talk to someone," Matthew suggested. "Your aunt. One of your friends."

"Too late. He's heading toward us. Dammit, I don't want to deal with him right now."

"You and me both." He hadn't had the pleasure of meeting Mr. Donovan yet, but he'd heard enough to already be wildly intimidated by the successful lawyer. Matthew knew his strengths, and he also knew that if Ernest Donovan wanted to discuss legal ideas, current events, or even great literature, Matthew was going to come across sounding like a goddamn idiot. *Shit.*

Why the hell had he said he'd do this? So far it had been easy—hell, it had mostly been Hannah. But

Ernest was the real test, and Matthew didn't think fast on his feet. Words always escaped him.

"Quick," Hannah said. "If we're already talking about something, he won't ask us about the engagement. Um, the school voucher system everyone keeps talking about. I think the Legislature's going to look at it again for Texas this year. What do you think about that?"

Terror ripped through him. He didn't have a clue about vouchers, and since he didn't have kids yet, he didn't have an opinion, either. Anything he said would reveal to Hannah that he was a clueless fool, and that was one thing he didn't want to be.

"Or you pick a topic," she said urgently. "Just talk. He's almost here."

But there was no topic. There was nothing for him to do.

Nothing except one thing.

He left the brisket on the table, pulled her roughly against him, and kissed her.

For a moment, she was stiff with shock. Then she melted against him, her mouth opening under his.

He sighed, lost in the feel of her. Because *this* felt right. Not overwhelming like the rest of it. *This*—the woman, the kiss, the pressure of their bodies —*this* was the way it should be.

And for one brief, delicious moment, Matthew knew what heaven felt like.

Chapter Seven

THEY'D BEEN MINGLING for at least half an hour when Hannah heard a familiar voice call, "There you two are!"

Matthew's incredible kiss had waylaid Ernest earlier, but now her stepfather was heading right for them, his voice carrying the several yards from where he stood in a group of gray-haired movers and shakers in law and business. Hannah recognized most of them—one had even been an adjunct professor when she was in law school—and they were all looking at Ernest as if he were the second coming of reason and virtue.

Maybe he was. Maybe he just got on her nerves because he'd replaced her father. Surely she wasn't so shallow as to find him irritating because he made her mom happy?

No, it was like she told Matthew—Ernest overshadowed her mom. Made her shift just slightly off center so that she wasn't entirely herself anymore. They were Ernest-Amelia instead, and that just made her sad.

Still, she didn't doubt that Ernest loved Amelia, which is part of what made it so hard to be around him. She didn't want to seem angry or ungrateful when he'd given her mom so much.

Now he was hurrying toward where they stood beneath a shade umbrella with his arms outstretched, and because she knew the drill, she moved into them for a bear hug. "Look at you, Hannah. You look lovely as usual. And you," he added, turning to extend a hand toward Matthew. "I'm looking forward to talking with you about your thoughts on a number of issues in healthcare and fitness right now."

She cringed as something like panic flashed in Matthew's eyes, but he rallied, and the relief that swept over her as he shook Ernest's hand was palpable. "That sounds great," he said. "But keep in mind that this is a celebration for you and Amelia. I'm not sure she wants to lose you to shop talk."

Ernest laughed heartily, and Hannah wanted to kiss Matthew right then. A thought that, surprisingly, wasn't even a figure of speech. Her cheeks burned from the realization of how much she'd enjoyed their earlier, unexpected kiss, and she looked down, trying to gather herself.

Which was why she missed Ernest's expression when Matthew said, "It really is a pleasure to finally meet you, Mr. Donovan."

Her head whipped up, and though Ernest's face was perfectly blank, she could see the shift from confusion to horror on Matthew's face. She opened her mouth to reply, but he got there first. And this time when she looked, his expression was nothing but calm.

"I am so sorry," he said. "Hannah speaks of you like a father and so I foolishly made that connection without even thinking, and it just slipped out."

"So you do know who I am," the older man said, the ego that Hannah knew so well obviously surfacing.

Matthew, she knew, had no clue.

"Of course he does," she hurried to say. "How can he be in business in Texas and not know——"

"Ernest Pierpont," Matthew said. "And Hannah is right. I can only hope that someday I make the kind of splash in the business community that you have."

Ernest chuckled, and Hannah forced a smile that she hoped looked completely innocent and not at all surprised. Next to her, Matthew cut his eyes toward her for just a moment, but she saw the satisfaction there and had to force herself not to laugh.

He'd talked to Selma or Easton, of course. And she gave him serious brownie points for doing his home-work. God knows she'd failed to properly prep him.

"Let me get you a whiskey," Ernest said, casually steering Matthew toward one of the drink stands. "Now, Hannah, you stay here. Let the men talk."

She swallowed, nervous, but Matthew only nodded.

And all she could do as they walked away was hope that Matthew stayed sharp. Because otherwise, they were screwed.

MATTHEW MANAGED NOT to hyperventilate throughout his conversation with Ernest, which, for the most part, was easily navigated. He'd obviously scored major brownie points for knowing Ernest's last name—thank goodness Selma had mentioned that the man was Hannah's stepfather or he never would have thought to run a Google search on the lawyer before Hannah arrived.

Fortunately, Ernest was prominent enough that his first name, town, and his wife's previous last name had been sufficient to track him down. One of Matthew's better attempts at research, actually. If he'd done as well in school, maybe he would have stayed past his sophomore year.

On the whole, the conversation with Ernest was easy. The man talked mostly about himself and very little about Matthew, a fact that seemed strange, but Matthew was grateful anyway.

It was only when Ernest cornered him later—after Matthew and Hannah had finally made it onto the dance floor—that the conversation turned truly odd. "You're in Hannah's room, of course," Ernest had said. "She never lived in it, but Amelia keeps her old things there, and we like knowing she has a place here."

Matthew only nodded, his feet starting to feel a bit leaden at the realization that he and Hannah were sharing a bed. Of course he should have thought of that earlier, but he'd never quite let his imagination go so far.

"To be honest, Amelia's old fashioned and would have preferred you sleep in separate room, but I told her this way was better."

"Oh, I don't want to upset Hannah's mother—"

"Nonsense. You're much less of an upset than the last time she brought ... someone ... with her."

"Sir?"

Ernest patted him on the shoulder. "We men have to stick together."

Matthew supposed they did, although he really didn't know what the man was talking about. Or at least he hadn't known. Later, as he and Hannah walked into the bedroom and he saw the double bed, it hit him.

"The last time you were here was with a woman."

She turned to him, her eyes wide. "So?"

He shook his head. "So, nothing. I just—something Ernest said just clicked with me."

"Oh." The tension that had seemed to fill her with his words fell away. "Yeah, he was less than thrilled about that."

"And your mom?"

"Remember what I said about her losing her identity?" She sat on the foot of the bed, then sighed. "Look, I'm sorry about this. I know sharing a room is super awkward."

He moved to sit next to her. "We'll survive." Hopefully, he sounded confident. The truth was, she was right. Simply sitting next to her was unnerving. He could remember the way she'd felt in his arms when the slow dances had come on. He'd been about to walk her off the floor, but she'd pulled him close, then whispered that her parents were watching. And he'd lost himself in the fantasy that she'd stayed because she wanted to.

"So, um, we should probably crash now." She nodded to a door. "That's the bathroom. You can go first."

He did, and when he came out in a T-shirt and

boxers, she looked up, startled from whatever she'd been reading on her phone.

"Oh." She said, and he stood there stupidly as her gaze skimmed over him, finally pausing on his face. Their eyes locked, and for a moment, he felt the warm heat from her attention bubble through him. Then her eyes widened, and she said, "Oh!" again, and a lovely blush crept up her cheeks, painting her pale skin red.

"I'm sorry. I didn't mean to stare. I only—well, holy hell, you know you're good looking."

She couldn't have said anything better if she'd tried. They both burst out laughing, and just like that, the tension evaporated. "I'm going to go change, too," she said when they'd calmed a bit. "Get into bed and feel free to make a pillow wall if you're afraid that I'm going to ravage that body of yours."

"I'll take my chances," he said, forcing himself to think of cold showers so that she wouldn't notice the effect that the threat of being ravaged by her was having on him.

As she'd suggested, he was in bed when she returned, though he hadn't built the pillow fort. He caught a glimpse of her in a tank top and sleep shorts, and all he could think of was how incredible it would feel to have those long, lean thighs wrapped tight around him. Never had he wanted more to make a pass at a woman, but he couldn't do that. Not under these conditions. In bed. Forced to share sleeping quarters. With her warm and soft beside him.

Fuck.

He rolled over, putting his back to her.

"Probably a good plan," she said. "Less awkward and tempting."

"Tempting?" he repeated, but was answered with only silence.

"Hannah?"

"I didn't mean to say that."

"Oh." He considered that, then found himself smiling. "I'm flattered."

"We've already established you're a hottie. Don't think you can go back to that well."

He bit back a laugh. "Fair enough." He shifted, then stiffened when her back brushed up against his. He closed his eyes, fighting for control.

"Small bed," she said, increasing the distance.

"Very." He cleared his throat.

She shifted again, and this time her foot rubbed his calf.

"You're doing that on purpose."

"Doing what to you?"

"I didn't say you were doing anything *to* me. I said you were doing *that*."

"But am I doing something to you?" Her voice was so low he could barely hear it, and when he did, he felt himself go even harder.

"Hannah…"

"I know. I'm sorry. It's just…" She rolled over, and he felt her breath against the back of his neck as her hand rested on his hip. "Well, it's just that I'm not interested in a relationship or any of the stuff we're pretending to be. But that doesn't mean I don't want you."

He closed his eyes. He should say no. He should slide away.

He should grab a blanket and sleep on the floor.

Instead he said, "What do you want?"

"Only tonight," she said. "We could call it method acting."

He swallowed the sudden lump that grew in his throat. "You're wearing barely nothing and you're pressed up to me in bed. If you don't mean what you're suggesting, you need to scoot away and not tease a man like that."

"Like this?" She slid her palm along his hip, up higher until her hand was under his shirt, and the heat of her palm against his skin was burning through him.

Slowly—wickedly, enticingly slowly—she moved her hand to his lower abs. Her body moved too, because she had to close the distance. Which meant that by the time her fingers had slipped under the band of his boxers, her entire body was spooned against him. Her chest to his back, her sex against his ass. Her breath against his shoulders.

He closed his eyes, striving for control but not finding it. He was hard already, painfully so, and when her hand slipped lower and curled around his shaft, she released a low, throaty gasp of pleasure.

"Tell me I did that. That thinking about me made you hard."

"Baby, you know it did."

"Do you like this?" Her hand was curved around him, and she stroked slowly with just enough pressure to drive him wild."

"God, yes."

"Me, too," she murmured, then shifted behind him, adjusting her position so that her lips teased his shoulder, his neck, his ear. And all the while she was teasing his cock, whispering about how much she wanted him. How much she'd wanted him the whole night.

"When you kissed me, I thought I'd come right then," she said, and that was when he couldn't take it anymore. He reached down to take her hand—mostly to make sure he didn't injure himself—and then rolled onto his back, forcing her to straddle him.

She grinned. "I like this," she said, then pulled off her top and tossed it onto the floor.

With slow motions, she freed his cock from his boxers, then moved her still-clothed sex over his shaft, now hard and throbbing against his pelvis. He tilted his head back, closed his eyes, and moaned. "I should be the one driving you crazy," he whispered.

"I'll hold you to that," she said. "Meanwhile, ladies first."

She bent forward, then kissed his lips. A soft buss before she started to slide down his body, her hips gyrating as her breasts rubbed against his T-shirt and her mouth sucked on his nipple through his shirt.

"Let me take it off."

"Hell no," she said. "But I'll take the rest of mine off." She rose on to her knees, and in what looked to be a truly acrobatic maneuver, managed to extricate herself from her sleep shorts without getting off of him or falling backwards. And when he saw that she wore no underwear, he sucked in a tight breath of air, all the more deep because she was so completely waxed that he could see ever sensual inch of her.

"Okay?" she asked, stroking her pussy over his rock-hard cock.

"Okay is an understatement." He had no idea how he was managing words.

She bent forward, a wicked grin on her lips. Then she moved her hips back and forth, sliding her slick heat all along his shaft until he had no choice but to arch his head back, close his eyes, and try his damnedest not to come.

That was a battle he was going to lose, but damned if he didn't want to be inside her. "Baby, have you got a condom? I didn't bring one." And wasn't he kicking himself for that. Sometimes it sucked trying to be a gentleman.

"I think I've got one in my purse. Maybe. I don't know."

She crawled off him, and he heard her dump the entire contents of her purse on the floor. Then he smiled at her squeal of triumph. "One," she said, then climbed back on the bed. "Make it worth it."

"I think I can promise you that," he said, thrilled by her delighted shriek when he took her by the shoulders, flipped her over, and straddled her.

Chapter Eight

"I WANT YOU UNDRESSED, TOO," Hannah begged. As decadent as it was to be naked while he still wore a shirt and boxers, she craved the feel of his skin against hers.

"Soon," he promised, then bent over her to capture her mouth with a kiss. She had no idea what he'd done with the condom she gave him, but she knew for certain that if he lost it she was going to be one very unhappy woman.

Then again, the way that he was sucking on her nipple while his fingers pinched its twin suggested that he knew a variety of ways to satisfy a woman. And oh, dear Lord, he was doing an amazing job at the moment. Just the sensation of teeth and suction, and she was pretty sure she'd come from this touch alone.

"Please," she murmured. "Don't stop."

He didn't, but he did slide his hand down between her legs, and in time with each long suckle of her breast, he thrust two fingers deep inside her, the rhythm driving her crazy until she was bucking against his hand, desperate for release, her mind too cloudy with passion to even beg for more.

"Christ, you're beautiful. Your skin flushed. Your body tight. That's it, baby. Come on." His thumb pressed against her clit and she arched up, coming so close to an orgasm that she whimpered in frustration.

He took pity on her and rolled them over once again, this time pulling off his shirt and nodding for her to tug off his boxers, which she did as quickly as she could. His cock sprang free, hard and ridged and beautiful, and she started to mount him, forgetting about the condom. He stopped her, sheathing himself, and then she lowered herself onto him, going slow to accommodate his girth, and then faster as her body molded to his.

She took his hand, putting his thumb back against

her clit, then arched back, riding him hard, as one hand teased her clit and the other cupped her breast, the pressure on her nipple tightening as the orgasm came closer and closer, until finally his thumb flicked over her clit just so and everything shattered.

Her core throbbed, her muscles milking his cock as he exploded inside her, and when he released her nipple and the blood flooded back, she had a second rush of pleasure cut through her almost as intense as the first.

"That was insane," she murmured, collapsing on top of him, then lifting her head long enough to kiss him.

"You're amazing," he said. "And as soon as I catch my breath, I'm going to roll you over, put my mouth between your legs, and make you come again."

She sighed with pleasure, her body shivering with anticipation. "I can live with that," she said, and his chuckle rumbled through her. "Except..."

She trailed off, then lifted herself onto one elbow.

"What?"

"It's just that—"

"I know," he said. "Only tonight. Method acting."

She exhaled. "I like you. Obviously. But I'm trying to build a business. I don't have time for a relationship. Or really even for hook-ups. There's too much mental energy, you know?"

"I get it."

"I don't want us to get in over our heads."

"We won't," he said. "We have a deal."

"But we're agreed about tonight," she asked. "Tonight, all bets are off, right?"

His eyes sparkled. "Roll over and spread your legs, baby. And I'll give you something to remember tomorrow."

HE WAS RIGHT, she thought as she sat down Sunday morning in the breakfast nook and dug into her mother's pancakes. She definitely remembered every delicious second of the night before.

Her body was gloriously sore, and she was wonderfully relaxed. Her only regret, in fact, was that there wasn't going to be a repeat performance.

They'd set down strict rules, after all.

"Good morning, beautiful," Matthew said as he joined her, looking incredibly sexy in khaki shorts and a Henley style shirt. He forked a few pancakes onto his plate. "This looks amazing. How long have you been up?"

"This is my mom's handiwork," she said. "Although I don't know where she—*oh! Mom*!"

Her mother rushed in, heels clicking, on the tile floor. "Sweetie, I have to rush. We have a church function this morning."

"But I thought we were going to talk about the money."

Her mother shot a glance toward Matthew, then curved her lips into a smile. "I talked with Ernest last night, and I think what you want may be possible under the new circumstances." She put a hand on Matthew's shoulder, then winked.

"Seriously?"

"But we can't talk about it now. Let us talk it over here, and I'll call you."

"But—"

"Drive home safe. It was so good to see you. Kiss-kiss."

"Mom!"

But it was no use. Her mother was click-clacking her way to the garage, and Hannah was left with no cash and an incredibly hot man who she'd banned from her bed.

She sighed and reached for the syrup. At last the pancakes were amazing.

Chapter Nine

FOR THREE FULL days after they returned to Austin, Hannah didn't have any time at all to think about Matthew. And yet somehow he managed to be constantly in her thoughts.

He was there during the hours when she and Easton were reviewing the lease one final time before they signed it on Monday, double and triple checking that the release clause hadn't been altered, and they could still get out from under the obligation if her mother didn't come through with the money.

He was there when they talked with the utility companies about hooking them up with phone and

Internet, and he was definitely there when they sat down at the library table and started talking about clients. Selma and Austin Free-Tail were on the list. And the first suggestion that Hannah made was to see if Herrington's Gym wanted to work with them as well.

Of course, Easton had already made contact with dozens of local businesses, and the two of them had meeting after non-stop meeting, sometimes retaining clients and sometimes setting up follow-up appointments.

They interviewed legal assistants, secretarial staff, and file clerks. And Easton started making calls to a few potential candidates to step in as the office manager.

Every night she went home exhausted.

And every night she fell asleep with Matthew on her mind. She'd even taken to walking the long way home to her condo, which took her down Lavaca instead of Colorado Street, simply because that's where his gym was located. The windows were tinted, but every once in a while the sun would hit at just the right angle, revealing a dim, almost film negative-like view of the interior. That happened once when she passed, and she caught a glimpse of him standing beside a leg-press talking to a woman who was nodding and sipping water. He paused, holding up his hand as if he were trying to catch a thought. Then he'd turned, as if searching for someone.

Her?

Had he realized that she was there?

She waited, telling herself that if he came outside it was a sign that they should have a drink or dinner. That they should forget their plan to ignore the chemistry between them and simply move on with their lives.

But he didn't step outside, and she'd kept going to her condo. Then continued on with her busy week. A week when she didn't have a single free moment that she could think of him.

And yet somehow she managed.

"So call him," her friend Shelby said, after Hannah rattled off the entire story one morning when they'd run into each other at the downtown Starbucks.

"Look who's completely changed her tune,"

Hannah said. "Nolan's been good for you. And you're welcome, by the way."

Once a completely straight-laced CPA, Shelby Drake had started dating Nolan Wood, a raucous drive time DJ with absolutely no filter. Hannah took full credit of course, since she was the one who'd convinced Shelby to buy sex toys as a bachelorette gift for a friend, thus sparking a chain reaction of naughtiness that had culminated with Shelby in Nolan's bed.

"I'm serious," Shelby said, pushing her glasses up her nose. "You obviously like the guy. Just call."

"I meant what I said to him. I need to focus on building the practice. I don't have time for a relationship."

Shelby pushed a lock of dark hair behind one ear, then sipped her latte. "Maybe not. But sounds like you want one."

Hannah frowned. She didn't. Truly.

But that didn't mean a few more non-committed hook-ups wouldn't be fun. Friends with benefits was a valid thing, right? And she definitely considered

Matthew a friend. Considering how well they got along, how could he not be?

That rationalization lasted all the way to the office. Then she got busy and reminded herself that this was why she didn't do relationships. Or, for that matter, hook-ups.

"It'll slow down," Easton said, leaning against her office door.

"What?" She'd been slouching behind her desk, but now she sat up straight. "I'm fine. Do I look like I'm complaining about the pace?"

He chuckled. "No. I'm just reassuring us both that we're in start-up mode. But it'll calm down."

"I'm not worried."

"Selma is," he said with a wry grin. "She made me promise to not work this weekend. And if I'm taking off, so are you."

She started to protest, but why? Her condo was a wreck. She could use the weekend to sleep and clean. Maybe even get a massage.

And see Matthew?

She frowned, shoving the thought aside.

"What's wrong?"

She smiled brightly. "Just debating between a massage or a body wrap. If you're making me blow off work, I'm going to do it in a big way."

"Good for you." He indicated the briefcase that he'd set at the floor by his feet. "I'm going to finish up at home. See you tomorrow. Casual Friday."

She rolled her eyes. She'd been on the floor going through file boxes most of the day, and she doubted the dry cleaners would be able to get the dust and grime off her favorite black linen slacks.

As soon as Easton was gone, she leaned back in her chair, trying to decide if she should stay or take some of her own work home with her. She'd just decided to go when her office phone rang, and she snatched it up. "Wallace and Donovan." God, she loved saying that.

"Doesn't that sound wonderful," her mother said. "Sweetie, I'm so proud of you."

"Proud enough to let me have the money from Daddy's insurance?" And wasn't she becoming bolder by the minute? She'd mentioned the money to her mom before she and Matthew had driven back, and her mother had intimated that it was certainly possible, but she needed to talk with Ernest.

"Why don't we talk about it tomorrow?" her mother asked, and Hannah's heart began to hammer in her chest.

"Tomorrow? We can talk now. I mean, I'm—"

"This calls for an in-person discussion and celebration. And Ernest and I will be in town, and we thought we should have dinner with you and Matthew to celebrate your engagement. We didn't get to chat with him nearly enough at the party."

"Are you saying you won't give it to me?"

"Sweetie, no. I'm saying we want to do dinner. Ernest and I were both charmed by Matthew. Seven o'clock? We can eat at Three Forks downtown. Matthew likes steak, I assume?"

"I—yes." She assumed so, too. "But—"

"Gotta run, sweetheart. Momma loves you."

"But—"

The line went dead.

Discussion? Celebration?

What did that mean? That the money was hers so long as she didn't screw it up? Which she wouldn't.

Or, rather, she hoped she wouldn't. It really wasn't up to her.

She needed Matthew again. And she really hoped he wouldn't say no.

Chapter Ten

HE SHOULD HAVE SAID NO.

Matthew paced the sidewalk in front of Three Forks on Lavaca in downtown Austin, checking and rechecking his watch. Hannah had said to meet her at six-forty-five so that they could chat before meeting her parents at seven. It was six-forty-eight.

He really should have said no. Seeing her again was … well, it was disconcerting. Or it would be if she showed up.

The simple fact was that she'd been on his mind constantly since the moment they'd parted ways after returning to Austin on Sunday. So much so that he'd even imagined seeing her on the street outside his gym, simply standing there and looking in at him.

He wanted her.

Damn, but he wanted her. But he also knew that she didn't want him. Not only had she made it clear that she wasn't interested in a relationship right now, but he knew damn well that at the end of the day a highly educated lawyer wasn't going to be interested in more than a fling with a glorified gym rat. And that was true no matter how pretty or convincing her words might be.

He checked his watch once more. Six-fifty.

He'd give her one more minute, and if she hadn't shown by then, he'd text an apology and he'd—

"Matthew!"

The power of the relief that flooded through him almost knocked him over, and he didn't even try to hold back his smile as she hurried toward him, looking completely put together in black slacks, a black blazer, and a white silk blouse. The complete opposite of the wild woman she'd been in bed. And honestly, both versions of her were equally appealing. There was nothing about Hannah Donovan he didn't find fascinating. Too bad she'd made it clear they shouldn't act on that attraction.

She'd obviously come straight from work, and though he had as well, he'd taken time to shower and change in the locker room. Now, he was wearing the same outfit they'd bought in Dallas. Not original, maybe, but it had worked once before.

She grinned when she saw it, then ran her fingers over the lapel. "Classy," she said, as he resisted the urge to reach out and touch her.

"You think he'll notice it's the same?"

"If he does, he won't say anything." She took a step back, then sighed when she looked up at him. "Thank you for doing this. It really is good to see you."

"Does this mean you're getting the money? Or is this the last test?"

"Honestly, I'm not sure. But I'm going to assume it's a test unless the first thing they do is hand me a check." She took his hand, then squeezed. "Okay?"

"You know it is," he said. "We put on this play once before. I guess this is our curtain call."

"The man likes theater." She hip-bumped him. "Maybe I'll talk you into taking me to a show."

He cocked his head, trying to decide if she was serious. "I have a friend with connections," he said. "I think I can score orchestra seats to pretty much anything you want."

"I guess that earns you points in the Keeper column," she said, but before he could study her face and get a read on her, she'd spun around in response to the quick beep of a car horn. With a wave, she hurried to the car stand, then greeted Amelia and Ernest as they left the car with the valet.

"So good to see you," Ernest said to Matthew, then began to wax poetic about a political luncheon they'd attended that afternoon to benefit an up-and-coming gubernatorial candidate. "Politics are a hideous business," he continued, once they were seated and the wine had been poured. "But once you're in the quicksand, it's hard to get out. How about you, Matthew? Any interest in politics?"

"Not particularly." He had a feeling that wasn't Ernest Pierpont's ideal response, but since there was no way that Matthew could fake knowing a damn thing about politics, it was the only answer he could give.

"I suppose not," Ernest said. "Not much need when you're an uneducated man running a gym, is there."

Matthew had been lifting his glass, but now he froze, his glance catching Hannah's panicked one.

"He's—"

"A gym owner, just like you said," Matthew put in, trying to keep his voice level and smooth. He took a sip of wine, mostly to let himself think. "I owe you an apology for misrepresenting myself. Hannah wanted to tell you what I do from the beginning, but I was nervous. She argued that I've supported myself since I was sixteen. That I started with a five-thousand-dollar loan from my parents and now have no debt and three established gyms in Austin, and even own the building downtown, which, frankly, is a prime piece of real estate."

He drew a breath, amazed that he was thinking and speaking clearly when his nerves were humming and his heart was pounding so hard it felt like he'd done a hundred-meter dash.

"She said that you'd respect me as an entrepreneur," he continued, not looking at Ernest's face, because if he did he'd surely lose his nerve. "That you'd see the same thing in me that you saw in Amelia—in how she worked her way up after being widowed as a single mother."

Beneath the table, Hannah's fingers dug into his thigh. He took another sip of wine, resisting the urge to look at Hannah. "She told me that a man like you—a man who understood people and business would respect what I've done. And after talking with you at your home, I realize that she was right. But before meeting you, sir—well, I confess that you intimidated me. And I made the decision to lie. To be the man I believed you wanted for your daughter, and not the man I truly am."

One more sip of wine. One more deep breath. And then he really did look Ernest straight in the eye. "I hope you can forgive me for underestimating you, sir. I assure you, Hannah never did."

"Well." Ernest leaned back, then looked between him and Hannah. "Well," he said again.

"My, my," Amelia said. "I can't remember the last

time I've seen you speechless." She winked at Matthew. "I think you impressed him."

"That you did, son." He turned his attention to Hannah. "You picked yourself a good man, Hannah."

"Yes," she said, with her hand still on his thigh. "I really think I did."

"That fifty grand is in a CD that doesn't come due for another year. But I've got fifty I can turn liquid by next week. We'll be back in town Wednesday evening. How about I bring you a cashier's check then?"

The hand on his leg tightened so much it almost cut off his circulation, but Hannah's facial expression never faltered. She kept calm, smiled, and thanked Ernest and her mother before lifting her wine in a toast to them.

She kept her hand on Matthew's thigh for the rest of dinner, only taking it away when absolutely necessary. And partly because of that—and partly because of the massive release of adrenaline after that speech, which qualified as the longest in his entire life, Matthew remembered absolutely nothing about the rest of the dinner except that he ate steak, had a bite of Hannah's cheesecake, and received a hearty pat on the back before Ernest and Amelia returned to their car and their hotel.

"We're heading back to Dallas before dawn," Amelia said. "But we'll see you next week when we bring the check to Hannah."

"Sounds great," Matthew said, hoping against hope that he developed a mild case of Ebola before then. Because honestly, he didn't think he could take a repeat performance.

"Hey," Hannah said as her parents' car pulled away. "Thanks so much for coming tonight. I was worried when Ernest called you out about the gym, but you turned it around beautifully. That was seriously impressive."

"And you're getting your money."

She grinned at him, her face lit up like a kid at Christmas. "I owe you big time for that."

"You would have gotten it eventually."

She shook her head. "Eventually is useless. Thursday is the last day we can back out of the lease and still get back the money we put down back. So knowing I'll have the cash on Wednesday and can tell Easton I'm truly in as a full partner? Well, it couldn't be more perfect."

He reached out and took both her hands, then looked into her smiling face. "It was my absolute pleasure."

"So, I was wondering…"

He cocked his head. "Yeah?"

Her cheeks turned a delightful shade of pink. "I just thought you might be thinking about asking me back to your place."

A warm rush of pleasure spread through him, and he regretfully shook his head. "Sorry. No."

"Oh." The depth of disappointment in her voice was probably the biggest compliment he'd ever received.

"I'm not going home."

"*Oh.*" Her brow furrowed. "Wait. I'm about to be really mortified, aren't I? Do you have a date?"

"Actually, yeah. She's five years old and as sweet as can be."

When she only stared blankly, he laughed. "I'm

babysitting," he said. "But you're welcome to tag along."

"MORE, PLEASE, MATTHEW. ONE MORE CHAPTER?"

Hannah stood inside the kitchen, just out of sight of the living room where Matthew was reading a *Magic Treehouse* book to five-year-old Faith, Brent Sinclair's little girl. An owner and head of security for The Fix on Sixth, Brent was also a single dad. Hannah wasn't sure if he was working tonight or if he had a date. All she knew was that Selma had been on deck when they arrived, and she'd flashed Hannah a thumbs-up sign when Hannah and Matthew had taken over babysitting.

Or, rather, when Matthew had. Babysitting wasn't high on Hannah's list of skills. Matthew, however, was a natural. A fact he proved as he negotiated with the little girl for another chapter, eliciting a solemn promise that bedtime would follow.

"Okay," he said when the chapter was over. "Now go run in and say goodnight to Miss Hannah. I bet you can even get a glass of milk from her."

Hannah smiled and went to pour the milk, then accepted the enthusiastic hug. Faith took the cup, downed a huge gulp of milk, then went running back to Matthew.

As the two of them headed to Faith's bedroom, Hannah brought a bottle of wine to the coffee table, along with two glasses.

"That's a good idea," Matthew said when he returned. He sat next to her and began to pour the wine. "Hard to believe someone so tiny can run you so ragged."

"You're really great with her," Hannah said.

"Well, she's a good kid. Brent's a lucky man. Except…"

She shifted to look at him better. "What?"

"It's just … well, I hope he doesn't stay alone for long. Other than that, his life looks a lot like the one I dream about."

"Really?" She shifted on the couch so she could see him better. "How so?"

"The full meal deal. Friends. A house. Kids. I want

a wife, but still, Brent's got a lot more of the puzzle in place than I do."

"You didn't mention your job."

"Oh, that's important too. I have to support them, right? But I'm not much of a businessman."

She thought about his three gyms around Austin and almost argued the point. But instead, she asked, "If that's what you want, then why aren't you dating someone? Or married, for that matter?" The question was sincere, but there was an emotion underscoring it that she almost didn't recognize. Relief that he wasn't involved with someone else? Jealously that the someone might not be her?

Seriously, what was going on with her?

She took a sip of wine to clear her head, then realized he hadn't answered the question. "Matthew? I'd like to know. Why don't you have a woman in your life?"

"Think of it as the opposite of what I told your dad. Most women want more than a high school dropout who can't even manage to keep three low-overhead gyms going."

She'd lifted her glass, but now she set it back down

again. "What are you talking about? I thought your locations were doing great? Hell, I thought you were thinking about franchising."

He sighed. "I'm making it sound more doom and gloom than it really is. My business is doing fine— it's only one location that's not pulling its weight, and I think I may have to give up on it before it brings down my overall bottom line."

"That sounds like a smart plan. Is that why you're not going to franchise?"

He shook his head. "My idea was to grow my business. And once I had three, I thought, why not franchise? Dozens, maybe even hundreds of Herrington Gyms."

"I'm not seeing a problem."

He lifted a shoulder. "I love what I do, but I want time that isn't just about my work. I want the family, too. The whole deal. And I'm not sure I can have that if I'm watching over a hundred gyms across the country."

"A lot of people make it work. Family. High powered careers."

"Maybe they do. But that's—well, honestly, I'm not most people."

"No," she said softly. She thought about all the attorneys and businessmen who traveled weekly and who wouldn't file a brief or a report without analyzing it or revising it to perfection. Had they put as much thought into their families as this man? "You're really not."

"What about you?" he asked. "Relationship? Career?"

"I haven't thought a lot about it, honestly. Except the career. I worked so long in a job I didn't love that I'm willing to spend the time to build up the practice Easton and I are putting together."

She took a sip of wine, then turned to him. "I guess I'm not as well-balanced as you are."

She thought he would laugh, but instead he just held her gaze. "I think you're pretty much perfect," he said softly.

"Oh." Their eyes locked, and she swallowed. Slowly, she put her glass down, then rested her palm on his thigh. He stiffened, and she was certain that he'd felt the shock of connection cut through him just as it had her. "Matthew," she said, but before the name even left her lips, he'd pulled her to him, closing his mouth over hers.

She swallowed a moan, opening her mouth to the kiss and her whole body to him. Flames kindled inside her, and she surrendered to him, wanting so much more. Hell, wanting everything he could give her.

He deepened the kiss, his palm on the back of her neck, his tongue tasting her, claiming her, until she thought she would melt in his embrace. Her body sizzled, craved, and when he gently pulled away, breaking the kiss, she almost cried out with frustration.

"We can't," he said. "Not here. Not while I'm babysitting." His eyes were dark with desire, and she could almost feel the desire rolling off him. Still, he shook his head, his breath coming hard. "We just can't. It's too damn cliché."

She wanted to argue—to tell him Faith wouldn't wake up—but she found herself nodding agreement. "If not now, when?"

She bit her lip, almost afraid he'd tell her the

answer was never. But to her immense relief, he said, "Go out with me tomorrow?"

"I—yes. Of course."

His mouth curved into a smile. "Good. I'll pick you up at seven."

Chapter Eleven

MATTHEW COULDN'T REMEMBER EVER BEING SO nervous for a date. Which was absurd, all things considered. After all, he knew even before he drove to her condo to pick her up that this was the kind of date that was for fun only. There were no expectations of a future. No hoping that something would develop.

This was about sex and attraction and nothing more.

After all, she'd made it quite clear that she wasn't looking for a relationship; she was putting all her energy into re-building a career that had gotten off track over the years.

He could respect that. Hell, he *did* respect that.

And yet despite his own rules about not dating if there was no chance for a future, he was as a nervous as a teenage boy taking a girl to the movies for the very first time.

Why?

Because despite her clarity, he still wanted her. Wanted to sizzle from that electricity that always seemed to arc between them. Wanted to talk and joke with her. Wanted to share the world with her, and then kiss her senseless and not think about anything at all.

Maybe he wasn't self-aware enough, but he honestly didn't know if he was giving in to his own desire and surrendering to the allure of a sexual relationship despite her assurance that there was no hope for a real future. Or if he was deluding himself into thinking that she'd change her mind. That she'd felt something real between them, too, and wanted to explore it.

He didn't know. And, damn him, tonight he didn't care. Tonight, he just wanted her. And there were real butterflies in his stomach when he rang the buzzer for access to her condo.

She opened the door with a smile so wide it sparked

his soul. "You look great," she said, her words echoing his thoughts. As far as he was concerned, he looked like he always did. Jeans. A tee. Nothing special. She, however, was a vision. She'd tied her hair back with a scarf, but loose tendrils had escaped to frame her face, giving her a carefree vibe that was accentuated by the knit sundress she wore that clung to her breasts and waist before flaring out in a swirl of material that flowed around her ankles.

"You're stunning," he said, delighted when her smile widened in response.

"Do you want to come in?"

"Actually, we're on a schedule."

"Yeah?" Her brows rose, but she didn't ask. Instead, she slipped on a pair of sandals and stepped into the hall, pulling the door shut behind them. Soon, they were back in his car and on their way to one of the docks beneath the MoPac bridge. He parked, then headed to the small wooden shack where one of his clients, José, stood waiting.

"Hey, buddy," José called. "You're all set."

"We're going out in a canoe?" she asked.

"Unless you're afraid of the water?"

She shook her head. "No, it sounds great."

"You picked a good night for it," José said, as he showed them to the canoe, which had a small ice chest already packed per Matthew's instructions, as well as a couple of blankets in case the early September night grew chilly.

"I'll lock her back up for you," Matthew said, and José nodded. Usually, he required the canoes to be returned by nine-fifteen. But Matthew had enlisted his friend in a different plan.

"Do you want me to row?" Hannah asked once they were in the canoe and on the river.

"I don't want you to do anything except sit back and enjoy."

She grinned. "I can do that."

When he was younger, he'd been in a rowing club, and he enjoyed falling back into the steady rhythm of moving the boat through the water. He knew the river intimately, and they moved leisurely toward the east and the Congress Avenue bridge.

"Do you know I've never done this before?" she asked.

"Why not?"

She shook her head. "No idea. I love it, though."
She looked around, glancing first toward the grassy
shores on the south and then to the trails, marsh,
and docks that dotted the more developed
north side.

The river—known as Lady Bird Lake now, but
Town Lake when he'd been a kid—marked Austin's
north-south line. Technically, it was part of the
Colorado River, but so were many of the Highland
Lakes up river, as they'd been created years ago by
either the Corp of Engineers or the Lower
Colorado River Authority.

However they'd been formed, the lakes—technically reservoirs—added to the beauty of the Austin
area and the Texas Hill Country.

"Do we have a goal?" she asked.

"I'm taking you to the place where Selma and I
used to go when we were kids. And hopefully, I got
the timing right…"

"Yeah? I'm intrigued."

"You'll probably figure it out," he said as he
steered the canoe close to the Congress Avenue

Bridge. "And it looks like we're right on time for sunset."

They weren't the only ones under the bridge. A larger boat that offered dinner on deck was moving slowly along the water, and a large flat boat full to the brim with passengers was also moving at a snail's pace.

They'd come, like Matthew and Hannah, to see the bats.

"You've seen them before?" he asked. Austin hosted the largest urban colony of Mexican Free-tail bats in the country, and the critters had become world famous. He doubted she could have lived in Austin and never watched them.

As expected, she nodded. "Several times. But never from the water."

"They live under the bridge," he said. "It's incredible to stand on the bridge and watch them rise up from under you. But from down here…"

He trailed off as the familiar sound began. A small squeaking. A hint of a flutter. And then, through some miracle of nature, they all seemed to wake at the same moment, and thousands of bats who'd been tucked in under the bridge, hidden in crevices or simply camouflaged, left their perches, fell into the open air, and then rose into the purple and orange twilight sky.

From their position in the canoe, half under the bridge, Matthew and Hannah saw it all. He heard her gasp as the cloud of bats swarmed out over their heads, and when he looked at her face, he could see the delight and the wonder.

"That was incredible."

"That's what Selma named her company after. Austin Free-Tail Distillery."

"And her Bat Bourbon," Hannah said, and Matthew nodded. She leaned forward and took his hand. "Thank you. That was amazing."

"We're not done," he told her, then maneuvered the canoe to a small dock that he'd discovered one day. It wasn't in the best shape, but it led to a secluded area in Zilker Park. He tied off the boat, helped Hannah out, then pulled out the ice chest and a blanket.

"I thought a nighttime picnic would be nice."

"That sounds amazing," she agreed as he pulled out

pasta salad and fruit, along with crackers, cheese, wine and candles.

They ate by candlelight, sipping wine and talking about their days. She told him about client meetings and statute of limitation issues and an appeal they'd been hired to argue. Her voice when she talked about the research underscoring how much she loved the work, which was enough for him. The actual legal discussion went completely over his head.

"I'm boring you," she said later, pouring him more wine.

"You're not. I'm just not fully on board with the question of whether or not some banking regulation is constitutional."

"Want me to explain?"

"Dear God, please no," he said, making her laugh.

"You know what I want to talk about?"

He laid back on the blanket and took her hand, expecting something sexy or romantic. Instead, she said, "The gym you're thinking about closing."

He rolled over. "You're serious?"

"Where is it? South Congress, right?"

"A couple of miles from here. Why?"

"Let's go see it."

His brows rose. "You realize you're completely changing the tone of my sensual and romantic picnic by the lake." Fortunately, his sister was Selma. And she could bounce from one topic and mood to another faster than anyone on the planet. So he was well-trained to handle wild shifts like this.

She kissed the tip of his nose. "Gyms aren't sensual? Can we walk there? Is the canoe okay tied up?"

"The canoe's fine. But I have a better idea." He helped her up, and they walked the few yards to the road. As they walked, he pulled up a ride share app, and within minutes, they'd been deposited at his South Congress location.

"This is a great space," she said once they were inside.

"I agree. But it's not drawing enough members to justify keeping the doors open."

"I bet it's your location. You're so close to all the shopping on South Congress, and that's geared mostly toward women. Not that women don't work out, but I wonder if this location wouldn't do better as something else."

"Which is why I'm thinking of giving up the lease."

"No, I don't mean leave it to someone else. I mean re-purpose it. You already have two solid gym locations with free weights and machines and personal training. But what if you make this location still be a gym, but switch it up? Spin classes and Pilates and yoga. That kind of thing. You know, draw more women in from the local retailers. Have a juice bar with a happy hour for after work. And twenty-minute classes for lunch breaks. What?" she added, frowning.

"Only that you're amazing."

"Yeah? You like that?"

He did. And it was a testament to his lack of business skill that he hadn't thought of it himself. But now that she'd suggested it, he could see the potential. "I like it a lot," he said, taking a step toward her. "You know what else I like?"

She grinned. "I can guess."

"I'd rather show you." He took her hand and pulled

her close, then crushed his mouth to hers before releasing her. "Take off your clothes."

She lifted her brows but didn't argue, and he watched as she stripped, then walked toward him, completely naked.

"Your turn?"

"Nope," he said. "I like this just fine." He nodded toward a bench press, and she didn't even ask what he wanted. Just laid back, her legs on either side, open and wet for him. So wet that he almost came right then.

"Scoot to the end," he said, then got down on his knees and buried his face between her legs. She tasted like heaven, and all he'd intended to do was get her off. But now his cock was aching, and he had to have her. Had to be inside her.

When he told her so, she moaned. "Yes. Oh, God, please, yes."

"On your knees on the mat," he ordered and she complied without hesitation. "Head down. Oh, baby." He cupped her ass, then freed his cock. This time he'd been smart and put a condom in his wallet, which he now retrieved.

He sheathed himself and slowly stroked the tip of his cock up and down, sliding along the sensitive area between her pussy and her ass.

She whimpered, and the sound made him harder. "Now. Please. Just fuck me now."

How the hell could he deny that? He used his fingers to ready her, then eased his cock in. She was so tight, and he was so ready, and as he pounded into her, he reached around and teased her clit, feeling her muscles convulse around his cock as she got closer and closer. Until finally—incredibly—she went over the edge, her body drawing his cock in so hard and tight that he lost his load at the same time that her knees gave out and she collapsed onto the mat.

"Wow," she said later as she rolled over and straddled him on the mat. "That was amazing. And we really have to clean this place up."

He laughed. "Yeah. We'll take care of that. Later."

"Good," she said, then rolled over and snuggled close, tucking her body against his. He sighed, so content that it made his chest swell. But, dammit, he couldn't let himself get too comfortable?

He started to rise.

"Matthew?"

"I'm sorry. But I—"

She rolled over and propped herself up on her elbows. "What is it?"

Shit. "I just—I know you're not interested in anything serious. I get it. I respect it. But knowing that ... oh, hell, Hannah. I don't want to let things between us get too comfortable."

"Oh." She sat up, hugging her knees to her chest. For a moment, she simply sat like that, naked and strong and incongruously vulnerable.

Then she met his eyes, hers full of something that looked like hope. "What if I'm okay with things getting comfortable."

He tilted his head, wary. "What are you saying?"

"I'm saying that I'm not writing us off. That maybe I want more than friends with benefits, or whatever we're calling this."

"Are you sure?" He couldn't quite wrap his mind around the idea that she'd want to explore some-thing permanent with him. She was off arguing about the constitution in courthouses. He was going to spend the next week trying to find the best price on spin bicycles.

Her brows rose a bit, then she grinned. "I am, yeah," she said as moved to straddle him, the feel of her naked body firing his senses. "Want me to prove it?"

And then, before he could even think about protesting, she leaned forward, her breasts soft against his chest, and kissed him.

———

HANNAH WASN'T sure how she pulled it off, but through some miracle of time management and stubbornness, she managed to not only blow through a significant amount of work at the office, but also to see Matthew each and every day well into the next week.

They'd checked out food truck fare in the evenings, taken long walks around the river, and watched the entire Liam Neeson action movie collection.

They'd also spent a ridiculously disproportionate time in bed at both her condo and at his house. And not in a relaxing way. Although she had to admit that their energetic sessions were definitely restorative.

And she couldn't remember ever mixing so many orgasms with so much laughter and heat. Because Matthew could go from making her giggle to making her fall completely, gloriously apart with more skill and humor than anybody she'd ever been with. He owned her completely, and she happily surrendered.

On Wednesday, she and Easton both cut out of work early to go meet Selma and Matthew at a small baseball field behind one of the schools in South Austin. "It's the final game in a tournament among foster kids," Matthew had explained. "Selma and I are both involved in an organization that sets up various activities for the kids and their foster families."

She hadn't realized that Matthew actually coached one of the teams, though considering how involved in fitness he was, she probably should have guessed. She ended up in the stands with Selma, cheering the team on.

"This is a great cause you guys are involved in," she told Selma as Matthew's team took the field.

"Well, it's important to us. We were in the system, so…" She shrugged, then narrowed her eyes. "You and my brother seem to be getting along."

"We are," Hannah said, but the words sounded flat and not nearly honest enough. She turned sideways to face Selma straight on, then leaned forward. "Actually, no. It's not just getting along."

Selma held her eyes, her expression unreadable.

Hannah drew a breath. In for a penny…

"The truth is," she said, "I've completely fallen for your brother."

For a moment, Selma only stared. Then a slow, easy grin spread across her face. "That's great news," she said. "Because he's head over heels for you, too."

Chapter Twelve

HANNAH HID a yawn behind her hand, then reached for the pitcher of Pinot Punch.

"Are we boring you?" Megan asked with a grin. They were at The Fix, waiting for the Man of the Month Contest to begin. Hannah and Megan were sharing one of the round tables with Selma, Easton, and Shelby, although Megan would be leaving soon to go do whatever it was she did during the actual contest.

Right now, she'd come over to tell Hannah that Matthew was in the back staging area and had wanted to send her a message. He'd sent her a scrawled note that said *Only you*, and it was now safely tucked in her back pocket. She figured she could use it to beat off any other women who might try to claim Matthew after he won.

Because, of course he was going to win. And that really wasn't just personal loyalty speaking.

"She's had a long day," Selma said, referring to Hannah's yawn. "We spent the afternoon in the sun at a softball game, and before that I'm pretty sure they wore each other out having wild sex. But I could be wrong."

Megan's face went beet red with suppressed laughter, and Easton patted Selma's hand. "That's my girl," he said. "No filter whatsoever."

Selma shrugged, completely unfazed. "Just telling it like it is."

And since she happened to be exactly right, Hannah didn't even try to deny it.

"Are you guys staying after for the premiere of *The Business Plan*?" Megan asked, probably trying to change the subject.

"That's the reality show about the contest and the bar, right?" Selma asked.

Megan nodded. "Brooke and Spencer finished the

renovations a few weeks ago, but they're still shooting the contest through to the end. But the first episode airs tonight and then it'll run weekly up to the end of the contest and a little beyond."

"I would love to see that," Hannah said sincerely. "But we're meeting with my parents after the contest. They're in town for some charity thing, and that's the only time they have to see us." It made her nervous waiting so late to get the check, but so long as she had it safe in her hands by tomorrow, all would be well.

"Too bad," Megan said. "By the way, how's your dad?" she asked Selma.

Hannah knew she was referring to Mr. Herrington, who Matthew had told her had suffered a heart attack while traveling.

"Doing incredibly well. They're taking a cruise back with lots of ports of call, and they've actually added time to it. He went to see a specialist in Prague and everything looks great."

Matthew had told her the same thing, and while Hannah was thrilled his father was fine, she wished his parents would return sooner, as she would love to meet both of them.

"That's terrific," Megan said. She was about to say something else, but the music started and Beverly Martin, an indie film star who was making a splash, took the stage to emcee the show. "Oops," Megan said. "Gotta run."

"Pretty cool watching this with Mr. September," Hannah teased Easton. "I wonder who would have won if you were up against my guy."

"It would have been a tie," Selma said, being loyal to both brother and boyfriend.

"Hell no," Hannah said, "Matthew would have whooped Easton's ass."

"Careful," Easton retorted. "Or I'll put you down for all of next month's court appearances and I'll stay in the office and write the briefs."

"I take it back. Your utter hotness would have decimated Matthew." She met Selma's eyes and shrugged. "What can I say? I'm a lawyer. I know how to lie."

Easton tossed a tortilla chip at her, but then the contest started in full, and they all fell silent.

One by one, the men paraded across the stage. Matthew was fifth, and as far as Hannah was concerned, he looked like sin personified. The crowd seemed to agree, because when he dramatically peeled off his shirt—then tossed it to a nearby table of screaming women—the whole place went wild. He smiled at the women, then searched the crowd, found Hannah, and winked.

"Oh, yeah," Hannah said, blowing him a kiss. "He's totally gonna win."

Later, as contestant number nine started down the red carpet, she shifted in her seat, trying to catch a server's attention. She didn't get that far. Because there, standing in the doorway and looking as cold as the tundra, was Ernest.

"Um, I'll be right back."

She hurried to him, certain he was overwhelmed by the raucous crowd. Honestly, who wouldn't be? The place was packed, and if you just wandered in…

She frowned, remembering that there was a doorman and tickets. "How did you get in?"

"We need to talk. Outside. Where I can speak without damaging my vocal cords."

She nodded, fear creeping up her body. She told

herself not to worry. There was nothing to be afraid of.

How wrong she was.

"That man," Ernest began, his voice tight, "is not for you. Bad enough that he has no education whatsoever, but to strip on stage? What the devil are you thinking?"

"No education? He *made* himself. What the hell happened between our dinner and now?"

"I did more research," Ernest said. "Saw his picture on advertisements for this ridiculous meat market."

"What? This contest is for a good cause."

"Cancer research is a good cause. Saving a bar is an excuse to get drunk."

"That is so not true. And what does it matter, anyway? It's not as if he works for you. And he's in fitness. Showing off how fit he is actually makes good business sense."

"But you being with him doesn't. I'm sorry, Hannah, but we need you to show better sense if you're going to take that money. Your father would want you to do better. So do your mother and I."

Fury spewed from her. "My father was a cop. He had a high school education and was dedicated to helping people. Do you even know anything about Matthew? My father would have adored him."

His steady gaze bore straight through her. "But he's dead, Hannah. And so we'll never know that for sure, will we?"

"Ernest—"

"Your mother and I talked it over. Find another man, and you can have the money. That's final."

He turned away, and she stood frozen to the spot as he disappeared in the evening crowd.

She didn't even realize she'd pulled out her phone and was dialing until she heard her mother's voice mail message announcing that she was away from her phone.

Dammit.

She sent a text instead.

No answer.

She waited.

Still no answer.

Her mother—her own mother—was ghosting her.

Easton found her standing frozen on the sidewalk. "Hey, you okay? He won. He was coming to look for you and got surrounded."

She licked her lips. "Told you."

"What's wrong?"

"I feel horrible. I—I already told my parents that we can't see them tonight. Can you tell Matthew for me? And congratulations. Just tell him I have to go home. I—I feel too sick to stay."

He studied her, his expression giving nothing away. Then he nodded and said simply, "I'll tell him."

As Easton went back inside, Hannah started walking home, hoping that she could make it there before the tears began to flow.

Chapter Thirteen

MATTHEW DIDN'T HAVE time to bask in his Mr. October title since he was too busy searching for Hannah in the crowd. But with the congratulatory handshakes and requests from women to sign various parts of their bodies with Sharpies, he was having a hell of a time finding her.

Twenty minutes later, he'd still had no luck, but he did find Easton. Or, rather, Easton found him.

"Welcome to the club, buddy," Easton said, making Matthew laugh.

"If it keeps this place open, I'm happy to parade around without my shirt." He glanced around. "By the way, have you seen Hannah?"

"That's what I came to tell you. She wasn't feeling well. Asked me to tell you she was heading home."

What the hell?

That wasn't like Hannah at all, a fact that made Matthew's worry rocket into the stratosphere. She'd be here for him tonight if she could. Which meant that she must feel worse than death.

"Did she go to an ER?"

"Just home," Easton said.

"Thanks. I'm going to go check on her." He clapped Easton on the shoulder as he passed, then kept his head down as he threaded his way to the front door, trying not to be rude, but at the same time working his way out of the bar as fast as he could.

It took another five minutes, but finally he was outside. He started to turn left, then remembered a nearby cafe that surely had chicken soup. Since Hannah probably needed something easy on her stomach, he turned right—and almost plowed straight into Ernest Pierpont.

"Ernest! Sorry. I didn't see you there."

"Obviously." The older man thrust out his hand, and Matthew took it automatically, only belatedly realizing that the handshake wasn't congratulatory.

It was a farewell.

"Sorry it didn't work out," Ernest said, pulling his hand free. "You may not understand that sometimes matches are about more than just attraction. There are other considerations."

"Other considerations?" Matthew repeated, as warning klaxons blared in his head.

"I don't want you thinking that I don't like you, son," Ernest said, ignoring the question. "For some other woman, I think you'd be quite the catch."

Matthew's head was spinning, and nothing seemed to quite make sense. "You're saying that you're not going to give her the money for the lease?"

"It's like I told Hannah. It's just not the right decision at this point. The girl needs to stand on her own two feet."

"You goddamn prick," Matthew said. "You steal her money and you pretend like it's all about her?"

"Now you watch it."

"No." Matthew took a step toward the man, all of his energy going to contain his fury. "You may be right. Maybe I'm not good enough for her. But that is her money that you've kept from her, making her jump through hoops and all sorts of other bullshit. You can delude yourself all you want, but this isn't about her. It's about you controlling her. Controlling Amelia. I know it. You know it. And most of all, Hannah knows it."

Ernest glanced down, and Matthew realized that he'd made a fist. "So you're going to hit me?"

"It crossed my mind," Matthew said.

Then he did the hardest thing he'd ever had to do in his life. He turned around and walked the other direction, his fist thrumming with the unfulfilled desire to smash in the smug son-of-a-bitch's nose.

HANNAH WAS on her third glass of wine when she heard the knock at the door. She cringed, afraid it was her mother. Or, worse, Ernest.

But when she looked through the peephole, relief swept over her, and she pulled open the door to reveal Matthew.

"Hey, sorry I bailed. I think I'm coming down with something." She glanced at the clock. "I'm surprised you were able to get out of there so quickly."

"I was motivated," he said, his smile thin. "I wanted to see you."

She frowned at him, certain something was off. Then again, maybe it was just her. She definitely wasn't having one of her best days.

He reached forward and felt her forehead, and the mere sensation of his skin against hers made her feel better. As if she could survive anything so long as he was beside her. As if Ernest and the money didn't matter a whit.

"You're not warm," he said.

"It's mostly my stomach." Not really a lie, since that's where all her angst was gathered, in her belly. She turned away, mostly so he wouldn't see the truth on her face, and he followed her into the living room. The half-empty bottle of wine was on the coffee table, and she mentally winced, hoping he wouldn't notice.

"I'm not sure wine is the best cure for stomach troubles," he said. "Do you want to tell me what's really going on?"

She sighed, then sat on the couch. "It's only—well, I've been thinking."

His face went blank as he sat on the edge of the coffee table facing her. "I'm listening."

"I've decided not to open the firm with Easton. He can find someone else to step in as a partner. He won't have any trouble at all."

She searched his face for a reaction, but he was obviously good at poker. The only clue that he was processing any of this was the way he tilted his head to one side, as if he knew that she was leaving something important out. He just didn't know what.

And if she had her way, he never would.

So she didn't have the money—that was fine. She could get another regular job. She could save up again. And she'd happily do that if it meant that Matthew could stay in her life.

But that meant that in no way could she tell him that her parents backed out—or that he was the reason.

"Why?" That was all he asked.

She swallowed. This whole moment was far too surreal. "I was thinking about your decision not to franchise. And I think what you said makes sense for me, too. If I'd started this firm when I was younger, I'd be all in. But I'm in my thirties. I should be thinking about other things, not about spending all that energy building a business. Does that make sense?"

"Baby, it makes perfect sense." He leaned forward to take her hands, and relief swelled through her. "It's also a complete lie."

She pulled back, or tried to. He kept a tight hold on her hands.

"You're sweet," he said. "But I'm not screwing this up for you. Talk to Brent. He's about as upstanding and stable as they come. Maybe he'll be a guy who'll impress your father."

"He talked to you." The words came out dull and heavy, as if she was in quicksand.

"I managed not to break his face. On the whole, I call that a win."

"Matthew—"

He rose. "No. You deserve your firm. I've watched you. Listened to you. I see how much you love the work. You deserve that life. And," he added, "I think Ernest is right. You deserve better than me."

In two long strides he was past the couch, heading straight for the door. She bolted upright then sprinted across the room, getting there before he did. "What the hell, Matthew?" The words spewed from her, thrust out from the emotion she'd been holding in all evening. "My stepfather decides I don't get the money. You decide I don't get you? Well, screw that."

"It's for the best," he said, then reached around her and opened the door. "I really am sorry." His words were like ice, frozen and hard.

And then he stepped over the threshold, and she felt her insides explode. "Fuck you, Matthew," she cried, trying to scream but only sobbing the words instead. "Fuck you," she whispered, then did the only thing that could give her any satisfaction at all

—she slammed the door in his anguished, pain-filled face.

Chapter Fourteen

SHE STAYED UP ALL NIGHT, but she didn't find a solution. How could she convince a man to love her? To stay with her? To support her?

She didn't know, and there was nothing tangible that she could do to make Matthew come back to her.

There *was* something tangible she could do about the money.

It was only five in the morning, but she showered, then pulled on her favorite pair of ripped weekend jeans and a Baylor Law School shirt that had been washed so many times that the *Res Ipsa Loquiter* transfer had mostly rubbed off, leaving only a few pale green splotches and the letters *ps*.

She slipped on her Birkenstock sandals, then headed out the door toward the office. It was Thursday, and the few people already on the street were mostly in suits or business casual. Didn't matter. As far as Hannah was concerned, it was the dead end of the week. Not to mention the dead end of her career.

It only took about five minutes to reach the corner of Sixth and Congress, and she was in the office by ten after six. Not surprisingly, Easton was already there.

"Hey," he called. "Is that you?"

"Who else?" They'd hired a receptionist and legal assistant, but since their official start time was nine, it would be a minor miracle if they had just traipsed into the office.

"I'm glad you're here. I wanted to talk to you about the meeting on Friday with the Banking Commissioner. I think I've come up with a decent argument for—"

"We need to talk."

He'd been talking loud enough to be heard in the

hallway. But now she was in his doorway, and she saw his eyes go wide when he saw her outfit.

"You're still sick? You should be home, not here."

"I'm not sick." She drew a breath, stepped into his office, and sat in one of his guest chairs. "You need to find another partner. Or cancel the lease. Or take it over on your own. I—I have to pull out."

He said nothing, just laced his hands behind his head, leaned back in his chair, and waited.

"Ernest told me last night I can't have the money. Apparently men who are on calendars aren't good enough for me. The bastard."

"The money isn't an issue, Hannah. I know you're uncomfortable borrowing from me, but we can pull it out of firm income. You can take a reduced draw every month until your share is repaid. Or we can talk to banks about getting you a loan. Hell, I'd happily sue Ernest and your mom for you. There are ways."

"We've talked about this. I'm not comfortable with any of those ways. If I borrow from the firm, you're taking all the risk. We both know I won't find another lender. I can't use my credit cards because that would be foolish with the interest rates. And the life insurance beneficiary was my mom. I'd never win a court battle."

"Maybe not, but if the press got wind of it—the baby girl denied the money her hero cop father wanted for her? With Ernest's position and power? We wouldn't even have to file. Just the threat alone."

She just shook her head. Thinking about suing her family was too much at the moment. "Please. Don't fight on this just because you like me. You need a solvent partner."

"I need a partner I respect and trust."

"I need Matthew. I—I want this. I do. But it's a lot of work. And I'm not sure I want it if I don't have him to support me."

It was the first time she'd voiced the thoughts that had been buzzing around in her head, but it was true. She understood the way he looked at life. Why he was cutting back instead of franchising. She understood it, and she respected it. But she still wanted to grow, even knowing how hard it could be. But she also knew it would be lonely. And she wanted Matthew beside her, filling the void. Maybe even giving her a family. One that they could raise together. One that gave her a reason for working hard.

She didn't say any of that aloud, but from the way Easton was looking at her, she thought that maybe he understood a little of it. Even so, she said, "I don't want this without him," just to make sure they were clear.

"You know I love you, Hannah. But sometimes you're a real idiot."

"Excuse me?"

"You do want this. And you want him, too. And you're not playing smart about either one of them."

"I—what?"

"Take what you want, Hannah. You want to be part of this firm, then do it."

"How?"

"I've already told you. Money's on the table. Use it. Pay me back a grand a month. Bring in a killer client and take it out of your share. Get your ass up to Dallas and tell your mother flat out how you feel. Threaten a lawsuit. All viable options. You say you want it, but you're not doing it. And you're making excuses for why not."

"Because—"

"*Not* because you feel bad about borrowing my money. You and I both know I can afford it. It's because of what you just said—you don't want to do it without him. I don't blame you. I don't want to do it without Selma."

"So—"

But once again, he wouldn't let her get a word in. "Fortunately, you're brilliant at arguing. It's why I want you as a partner."

"I am good," she said. "But that's the problem. Matthew doesn't think he's good enough for me. He thinks I'm some intellectual icon and he's a gutter rat. It's ridiculous, but it's in his head."

"So you convince him."

"What if I can't?"

"Then I guess you're out of options. So I suggest you try really hard."

Chapter Fifteen

IT WAS one in the morning by the time Hannah got her courage up, but she didn't care. She stood on his front porch and pounded on the front door, alternating her violent knocks with equally harsh stabs at his doorbell.

Finally, a light flipped on inside, and she took one step back, waiting for the door to open. As soon as it did, she rushed inside, the finger that was on the doorbell now punching like a drill press against his chest.

"Was it all just a game to you? The time we spent together? Everything we said? Everything we did?"

"Hi, Hannah," he said sleepily. "What the hell?"

"You heard me." She shoved him with her palms. "Wake up and tell me. Were we just some game you played?"

He scrubbed his hands over his face, then looked at her with such conviction it made her take a step back. "No. Never a game."

"Then what?"

"A fantasy," he said. "For both of us."

He sighed, then dragged his hands through his hair before flopping down onto the couch and nodding for her to do the same. She stayed standing.

"You're still living in that fantasy land if you think we can work," he said. "Your stepfather had it right. You're champagne and caviar, and I'm beer and barbecue."

"I like beer and barbecue," she said, wishing she could get inside his head and make him understand.

"Who doesn't? But only for a while. Not forever. You have a good life. You're going to do good things. Important things."

"Dammit, Matthew, you have the thickest head. Don't you see? I will do those things. But it won't be right unless you're there to hold my hand. You're the person who makes me whole. The person who helps me to see—and to be—who I really am. I wasn't looking for you, but I found you. And now I need you."

"You don't," he said, then he stood and pulled her close, kissing her with such fierce passion that she was certain that when they broke apart he would tell her it was all a joke, and of course he was staying with her.

But when he stepped back, all he did was nod toward the door and say, "I think it's time for you to go."

Fight for him. Argue to win him.

But what else was there to say?

She nodded, then moved to the door. With her hand on the knob, she turned back to him. "Just think it over, okay? Don't screw this up for us. We've barely gotten started. I think we're real. And honestly, I thought that you did, too."

REAL.

The word cut through the hum that had been filling his head since Wednesday night. A fog that sounded remarkably like Ernest Pierpont telling him that he was worthless.

But here was Hannah telling him the opposite. And she was the one he wanted to believe.

Wanted, yes. But he also didn't want to derail her life or her ambitions. If he was going to be with her, he wanted to be an asset, a partner, an equal. Definitely not a burden.

So what was real?

Her hand turned on the knob, and he snapped. He couldn't let her leave—not like this. He lunged, taking her wrist and pulling her toward him.

All he meant to do was tell her to stay, but she was in his arms, her breath coming hard. He couldn't resist one last taste, and when he closed his mouth over hers, she melted against him. He lost himself in the kiss. In the knowledge that she was right. *This* was real. Them. Together.

"Hannah," he said when they finally broke apart.

"Don't you dare tell me again that you're not good enough. I don't want to hear it. You're the best man I know. You'll be the best father I can imagine. And I don't want to work my tail off building a law firm unless I'm doing it for a reason."

She cupped his cheek. "Don't you see that you're the reason? That I want to have a future with you. Or, at least, I want us to try. I don't want to scare you away, but I'm falling in love with you. If you're going to break my heart, do it now and I'll leave. But if we have a chance..."

His heart ached for her, and in his mind he saw that future. Him working his gyms. A boy on a soccer field. A girl on the high dive. His wife in the stands beside him cheering them on. Probably with a red pencil and a legal brief beside her.

The image made him smile.

"What?"

"Just promise me one thing."

"Sure."

"No taking work to the kids' competitions."

She stared at him as if he'd gone crazy, then she burst out laughing. "I think I can promise that. So long as you promise to never make me run a marathon with you."

"Deal."

They grinned at each other, and he thought that he could probably run two marathons right then.

Her grin turned impish. "Shall we seal it with a kiss?"

"I've got a better idea," he said, as he pulled off his shirt and tossed it to the ground. "Take off your clothes."

Her brows rose. "Really? Why?"

"Nudity's a great equalizer," he said matter-of-factly. "But mostly, that's how I want to seal this deal with the woman I love."

"I can live with that," she said, as she pulled her T-shirt over her head and then slid into his arms.

LATER, naked and sated, he held her close in bed and let the rhythm of her heartbeat echo through him as he wondered how in the hell he'd gotten so lucky.

Then again, luck was relative. And though he'd won Hannah, she'd lost out, at least as far as her dad's money was concerned. "Are you just going to let it go?"

"For a little while," she said, obviously understanding that he meant the money. "I'll ask again in a few months. And if the answer is still no ... well, Easton has an idea that I'm pretty sure will work. And then I—*we*—can take that money and put it away for our own kids," she added, her words giving him a special kind of glow.

She rolled over to face him, their legs twined as she snuggled close. "Hopefully Mom will come around before I have to sic Easton on her. But right now, it doesn't matter. Right now, I've got everything I need."

He held her tight, not quite believing this was real, and yet at the same time, certain nothing in his life had been more perfect.

"Yeah," he said with all his heart. "Me, too."

Epilogue

BEVERLY MARTIN PUSHED a strand of hair out of her eyes as she leaned over Griffin's shoulder so they could both see the computer screen.

"I don't think Angelique would argue with Hammond right now," she said, reaching over him to tap the screen.

She had to lean forward to do that, and she caught the freshly washed scent of his ever-present hoodie and breathed deep. He still wore it constantly around her, despite the fact that they'd been working together for months, pulling long hours on the revisions to Griffin's screenplay that was set to go into production soon, assuming the stars stayed in alignment.

"You may be right," he said. "She's not going to show her cards yet."

"Exactly." She moved her hand away so that he could see the screen, resting it now on his right shoulder. She felt the hard, rigged scar tissue beneath his T-shirt and hoodie. And she also felt his muscles tense.

"Beverly."

"Yes, that line," she said, pretending to misunderstand.

"Beverly, don't."

"Don't what?"

For a moment, he was silent. "You know."

She waited a beat, then another. Then she lifted her hand off his shoulder. But, dammit, this was getting ridiculous. She couldn't be in the same room with him without fighting her way through an electrical storm of attraction, all the more intense because he never let lightning strike. Which was a stupid metaphor, but that only proved how much he was messing with her mind.

Time to take a stand.

She moved around his chair, then leaned against the desk so that she was facing him, the computer at her back, and Griffin right in front of her. That close, there was no way she could avoid seeing the massive scars that marred the right side of his face. Of his entire body, she believed, though she'd never actually seen as much.

"Beverly." Her name was a growl, and he tilted his head down, putting his face in shadows.

"Dammit, Griff. What the hell is wrong with you?"

"Wrong with me?" His head jerked up, his voice filled with anger and derision. "Take a goddamn look."

"I've been looking for months," she retorted. "I don't see a thing."

"Do *not* patronize me."

"You're an idiot. You know that?"

He rolled his chair backwards. "We're done for today."

She grabbed the arms and pulled it back. "No, we're not." She closed her hand over his right one, the rough, destroyed flesh hard beneath her palm.

For a moment, their eyes met, then he looked away.

She took a breath for courage, then lifted her hand, moving it to his hoodie. Gently, she pushed it off his head.

"Don't," he said, his voice tight.

"Then stop me," she said, cupping her palm over his scarred cheek. She met his eyes again, her heart pounding as she waited for him to do just that. And then, when he stayed motionless, she did what she had wanted to do for ages. She bent forward, closed her mouth over his, and kissed him.

Are you eager to learn which Man of the Month book features which sexy hero? Here's a handy list!

Down On Me - meet Reece
Hold On Tight - meet Spencer
Need You Now - meet Cameron
Start Me Up - meet Nolan
Get It On - meet Tyree
In Your Eyes - meet Parker
Turn Me On - meet Derek
Shake It Up - meet Landon
All Night Long - meet Easton
In Too Deep - meet Matthew
Light My Fire - meet Griffin
Walk The Line - meet Brent
&
Bar Bites: A Man of the Month Cookbook

Down On Me excerpt

Did you miss book one in the Man of the Month series? Here's an excerpt from Down On Me!

Chapter One

Reece Walker ran his palms over the slick, soapy ass of the woman in his arms and knew that he was going straight to hell.

Not because he'd slept with a woman he barely knew. Not because he'd enticed her into bed with a series of well-timed bourbons and particularly inventive half-truths. Not even because he'd lied to his best friend Brent about why Reece couldn't drive with him to the airport to pick up Jenna, the third player in their trifecta of lifelong friendship.

No, Reece was staring at the fiery pit because he was a lame, horny asshole without the balls to tell the naked beauty standing in the shower with him that she wasn't the woman he'd been thinking about for the last four hours.

And if that wasn't one of the pathways to hell, it damn sure ought to be.

He let out a sigh of frustration, and Megan tilted her head, one eyebrow rising in question as she slid her hand down to stroke his cock, which was demonstrating no guilt whatsoever about the whole going to hell issue. "Am I boring you?"

"Hardly." That, at least, was the truth. He felt like a prick, yes. But he was a well-satisfied one. "I was just thinking that you're beautiful."

She smiled, looking both shy and pleased—and Reece felt even more like a heel. What the devil was wrong with him? She *was* beautiful. And hot and funny and easy to talk to. Not to mention good in bed.

But she wasn't Jenna, which was a ridiculous comparison. Because Megan qualified as fair game, whereas Jenna was one of his two best friends. She trusted him. Loved him. And despite the way his cock perked up at the thought of doing all sorts of delicious things with her in bed, Reece knew damn well that would never happen. No way was he risking their friendship. Besides, Jenna didn't love him like that. Never had, never would.

And that—plus about a billion more reasons—meant that Jenna was entirely off-limits.

Too bad his vivid imagination hadn't yet gotten the memo.

Fuck it.

He tightened his grip, squeezing Megan's perfect rear. "Forget the shower," he murmured. "I'm taking you back to bed." He needed this. Wild. Hot. Demanding. And dirty enough to keep him from thinking.

Hell, he'd scorch the earth if that's what it took to burn Jenna from his mind—and he'd leave Megan limp, whimpering, and very, very satisfied. His guilt. Her pleasure. At least it would be a win for one of them.

And who knows? Maybe he'd manage to fuck the fantasies of his best friend right out of his head.

It didn't work.

Reece sprawled on his back, eyes closed, as Megan's gentle fingers traced the intricate outline of the tattoos inked across his pecs and down his arms. Her touch was warm and tender, in stark contrast to the way he'd just fucked her—a little too wild, a little too hard, as if he were fighting a battle, not making love.

Well, that was true, wasn't it?

But it was a battle he'd lost. Victory would have brought oblivion. Yet here he was, a naked woman beside him, and his thoughts still on Jenna, as wild and intense and impossible as they'd been since that night eight months ago when the earth had shifted beneath him, and he'd let himself look at her as a woman and not as a friend.

One breathtaking, transformative night, and Jenna didn't even realize it. And he'd be damned if he'd ever let her figure it out.

Beside him, Megan continued her exploration, one fingertip tracing the outline of a star. "No names? No wife or girlfriend's initials hidden in the design?"

He turned his head sharply, and she burst out laughing.

"Oh, don't look at me like that." She pulled the sheet up to cover her breasts as she rose to her knees beside him. "I'm just making conversation. No hidden agenda at all. Believe me, the last thing I'm interested in is a relationship." She scooted away, then sat on the edge of the bed, giving him an enticing view of her bare back. "I don't even do overnights."

As if to prove her point, she bent over, grabbed her bra off the floor, and started getting dressed.

"Then that's one more thing we have in common." He pushed himself up, rested his back against the headboard, and enjoyed the view as she wiggled into her jeans.

"Good," she said, with such force that he knew she meant it, and for a moment he wondered what had soured her on relationships.

As for himself, he hadn't soured so much as fizzled. He'd had a few serious girlfriends over the years, but it never worked out. No matter how good it started, invariably the relationship crumbled. Eventually, he had to acknowledge that he simply wasn't relationship material. But that didn't mean he was a monk, the last eight months notwithstanding.

She put on her blouse and glanced around, then slipped her feet into her shoes. Taking the hint, he got up and pulled on his jeans and T-shirt. "Yes?" he asked, noticing the way she was eying him speculatively.

"The truth is, I was starting to think you might be in a relationship."

"What? Why?"

She shrugged. "You were so quiet there for a while, I wondered if maybe I'd misjudged you. I thought you might be married and feeling guilty."

Guilty.

The word rattled around in his head, and he groaned. "Yeah, you could say that."

"Oh, *hell*. Seriously?"

"No," he said hurriedly. "Not that. I'm not cheating on my non-existent wife. I wouldn't. Not ever." Not in small part because Reece wouldn't ever have a wife since he thought the institution of marriage was a crock, but he didn't see the need to explain that to Megan.

"But as for guilt?" he continued. "Yeah, tonight I've got that in spades."

She relaxed slightly. "Hmm. Well, sorry about the guilt, but I'm glad about the rest. I have rules, and I consider myself a good judge of character. It makes me cranky when I'm wrong."

"Wouldn't want to make you cranky."

"Oh, you really wouldn't. I can be a total bitch." She sat on the edge of the bed and watched as he tugged on his boots. "But if you're not hiding a wife in your attic, what are you feeling guilty about? I assure you, if it has anything to do with my satisfaction, you needn't feel guilty at all." She flashed a mischievous grin, and he couldn't help but smile back. He hadn't invited a woman into his bed for eight long months. At least he'd had the good fortune to pick one he actually liked.

"It's just that I'm a crappy friend," he admitted.

"I doubt that's true."

"Oh, it is," he assured her as he tucked his wallet into his back pocket. The irony, of course, was that as far as Jenna knew, he was an excellent friend. The best. One of her two pseudo-brothers with whom she'd sworn a blood oath the summer after sixth grade, almost twenty years ago.

From Jenna's perspective, Reece was at least as good as Brent, even if the latter scored bonus points because he was picking Jenna up at the airport while Reece was trying to fuck his personal demons into oblivion. Trying anything, in fact, that would exorcise the memory of how she'd clung to him that night, her curves enticing and her breath intoxicating, and not just because of the scent of too much alcohol.

She'd trusted him to be the white knight, her noble rescuer, and all he'd been able to think about was the feel of her body, soft and warm against his, as he carried her up the stairs to her apartment.

A wild craving had hit him that night, like a tidal wave of emotion crashing over him, washing away the outer shell of friendship and leaving nothing but raw desire and a longing so potent it nearly brought him to his knees.

It had taken all his strength to keep his distance when the only thing he'd wanted was to cover every inch of her naked body with kisses. To stroke her skin and watch her writhe with pleasure.

He'd won a hard-fought battle when he reined in his desire that night. But his victory wasn't without its wounds. She'd pierced his heart when she'd drifted to sleep in his arms, whispering that she loved him—and he knew that she meant it only as a friend.

More than that, he knew that he was the biggest asshole to ever walk the earth.

Thankfully, Jenna remembered nothing of that night. The liquor had stolen her memories, leaving her with a monster hangover, and him with a Jenna-shaped hole in his heart.

"Well?" Megan pressed. "Are you going to tell me? Or do I have to guess?"

"I blew off a friend."

"Yeah? That probably won't score you points in the Friend of the Year competition, but it doesn't sound too dire. Unless you were the best man and blew off the wedding? Left someone stranded at the side of the road somewhere in West Texas? Or promised to feed their cat and totally forgot? Oh, God. Please tell me you didn't kill Fluffy."

He bit back a laugh, feeling slightly better. "A friend came in tonight, and I feel like a complete shit for not meeting her plane."

"Well, there are taxis. And I assume she's an adult?"

"She is, and another friend is there to pick her up."

"I see," she said, and the way she slowly nodded suggested that she saw too much. "I'm guessing that *friend* means *girlfriend*? Or, no. You wouldn't do that. So she must be an ex."

"Really not," he assured her. "Just a friend. Lifelong, since sixth grade."

"Oh, I get it. Longtime friend. High expectations. She's going to be pissed."

"Nah. She's cool. Besides, she knows I usually work nights."

"Then what's the problem?"

He ran his hand over his shaved head, the bristles from the day's growth like sandpaper against his palm. "Hell if I know," he lied, then forced a smile, because whether his problem was guilt or lust or just plain stupidity, she hardly deserved to be on the receiving end of his bullshit.

He rattled his car keys. "How about I buy you one last drink before I take you home?"

"You're sure you don't mind a working drink?" Reece asked as he helped Megan out of his cherished baby blue vintage Chevy pickup. "Normally I wouldn't take you to my job, but we just hired a new bar back, and I want to see how it's going."

He'd snagged one of the coveted parking spots on Sixth Street, about a block down from The Fix, and he glanced automatically toward the bar, the glow from the windows relaxing him. He didn't own the place, but it was like a second home to him and had been for one hell of a long time.

"There's a new guy in training, and you're not there? I thought you told me you were the manager?"

"I did, and I am, but Tyree's there. The owner, I mean. He's always on site when someone new is starting. Says it's his job, not mine. Besides,

Sunday's my day off, and Tyree's a stickler for keeping to the schedule."

"Okay, but why are you going then?"

"Honestly? The new guy's my cousin. He'll probably give me shit for checking in on him, but old habits die hard." Michael had been almost four when Vincent died, and the loss of his dad hit him hard. At sixteen, Reece had tried to be stoic, but Uncle Vincent had been like a second father to him, and he'd always thought of Mike as more brother than cousin. Either way, from that day on, he'd made it his job to watch out for the kid.

"Nah, he'll appreciate it," Megan said. "I've got a little sister, and she gripes when I check up on her, but it's all for show. She likes knowing I have her back. And as for getting a drink where you work, I don't mind at all."

As a general rule, late nights on Sunday were dead, both in the bar and on Sixth Street, the popular downtown Austin street that had been a focal point of the city's nightlife for decades. Tonight was no exception. At half-past one in the morning, the street was mostly deserted. Just a few cars moving slowly, their headlights shining toward the west, and a smattering of couples, stumbling and laughing. Probably tourists on their way back to one of the downtown hotels.

It was late April, though, and the spring weather was drawing both locals and tourists. Soon, the area —and the bar—would be bursting at the seams. Even on a slow Sunday night.

Situated just a few blocks down from Congress Avenue, the main downtown artery, The Fix on Sixth attracted a healthy mix of tourists and locals. The bar had existed in one form or another for decades, becoming a local staple, albeit one that had been falling deeper and deeper into disrepair until Tyree had bought the place six years ago and started it on much-needed life support.

"You've never been here before?" Reece asked as he paused in front of the oak and glass doors etched with the bar's familiar logo.

"I only moved downtown last month. I was in Los Angeles before."

The words hit Reece with unexpected force. Jenna had been in LA, and a wave of both longing and regret crashed over him. He should have gone with Brent. What the hell kind of friend was he, punishing Jenna because he couldn't control his own damn libido?

With effort, he forced the thoughts back. He'd already beaten that horse to death.

"Come on," he said, sliding one arm around her shoulder and pulling open the door with his other. "You're going to love it."

He led her inside, breathing in the familiar mix of alcohol, southern cooking, and something indiscernible he liked to think of as the scent of a damn good time. As he expected, the place was mostly empty. There was no live music on Sunday nights, and at less than an hour to closing, there were only three customers in the front room.

"Megan, meet Cameron," Reece said, pulling out a stool for her as he nodded to the bartender in introduction. Down the bar, he saw Griffin Draper, a regular, lift his head, his face obscured by his hoodie, but his attention on Megan as she chatted with Cam about the house wines.

Reece nodded hello, but Griffin turned back to his notebook so smoothly and nonchalantly that Reece wondered if maybe he'd just been staring into space, thinking, and hadn't seen Reece or Megan at all. That was probably the case, actually. Griff wrote a popular podcast that had been turned into an even more popular web series, and when he wasn't recording the dialogue, he was usually writing a script.

"So where's Mike? With Tyree?"

Cameron made a face, looking younger than his twenty-four years. "Tyree's gone."

"You're kidding. Did something happen with Mike?" His cousin was a responsible kid. Surely he hadn't somehow screwed up his first day on the job.

"No, Mike's great." Cam slid a Scotch in front of Reece. "Sharp, quick, hard worker. He went off the clock about an hour ago, though. So you just missed him."

"Tyree shortened his shift?"

Cam shrugged. "Guess so. Was he supposed to be on until closing?"

"Yeah." Reece frowned. "He was. Tyree say why he cut him loose?"

"No, but don't sweat it. Your cousin's fitting right in. Probably just because it's Sunday and slow. " He made a face. "And since Tyree followed him out, guess who's closing for the first time alone."

"So you're in the hot seat, huh? " Reece tried to sound casual. He was standing behind Megan's stool, but now he moved to lean against the bar, hoping his casual posture suggested that he wasn't worried at all. He was, but he didn't want Cam to realize it. Tyree didn't leave employees to close on their own. Not until he'd spent weeks training them.

"I told him I want the weekend assistant manager position. I'm guessing this is his way of seeing how I work under pressure."

"Probably," Reece agreed half-heartedly. "What did he say?"

"Honestly, not much. He took a call in the office, told Mike he could head home, then about fifteen minutes later said he needed to take off, too, and that I was the man for the night."

"Trouble?" Megan asked.

"No. Just chatting up my boy," Reece said, surprised at how casual his voice sounded. Because the scenario had trouble printed all over it. He just wasn't sure what kind of trouble.

He focused again on Cam. "What about the wait-staff?" Normally, Tiffany would be in the main bar taking care of the customers who sat at tables. "He didn't send them home, too, did he?"

"Oh, no," Cam said. "Tiffany and Aly are scheduled to be on until closing, and they're in the back with—"

But his last words were drowned out by a high-pitched squeal of "*You're here!*" and Reece looked up to find Jenna Montgomery—the woman he craved —barreling across the room and flinging herself into his arms.

Meet Damien Stark

Only his passion could set her free…

Release Me
Claim Me
Complete Me
Anchor Me
Lost With Me

Meet Damien Stark in Release Me, *book 1 of the wildly sensual series that's left millions of readers breathless …*

Chapter One

A cool ocean breeze caresses my bare shoulders,

and I shiver, wishing I'd taken my roommate's advice and brought a shawl with me tonight. I arrived in Los Angeles only four days ago, and I haven't yet adjusted to the concept of summer temperatures changing with the setting of the sun. In Dallas, June is hot, July is hotter, and August is hell.

Not so in California, at least not by the beach. LA Lesson Number One: Always carry a sweater if you'll be out after dark.

Of course, I could leave the balcony and go back inside to the party. Mingle with the millionaires. Chat up the celebrities. Gaze dutifully at the paintings. It is a gala art opening, after all, and my boss brought me here to meet and greet and charm and chat. Not to lust over the panorama that is coming alive in front of me. Bloodred clouds bursting against the pale orange sky. Blue-gray waves shimmering with dappled gold.

I press my hands against the balcony rail and lean forward, drawn to the intense, unreachable beauty of the setting sun. I regret that I didn't bring the battered Nikon I've had since high school. Not that it would have fit in my itty-bitty beaded purse. And a bulky camera bag paired with a little black dress is a big, fat fashion no-no.

But this is my very first Pacific Ocean sunset, and I'm determined to document the moment. I pull out my iPhone and snap a picture.

"Almost makes the paintings inside seem redundant, doesn't it?" I recognize the throaty, feminine voice and turn to face Evelyn Dodge, retired actress turned agent turned patron of the arts—and my hostess for the evening.

"I'm so sorry. I know I must look like a giddy tourist, but we don't have sunsets like this in Dallas."

"Don't apologize," she says. "I pay for that view every month when I write the mortgage check. It damn well better be spectacular."

I laugh, immediately more at ease.

"Hiding out?"

"Excuse me?"

"You're Carl's new assistant, right?" she asks, referring to my boss of three days.

"Nikki Fairchild."

"I remember now. Nikki from Texas." She looks me up and down, and I wonder if she's disappointed that I don't have big hair and cowboy boots. "So who does he want you to charm?"

"Charm?" I repeat, as if I don't know exactly what she means.

She cocks a single brow. "Honey, the man would rather walk on burning coals than come to an art show. He's fishing for investors and you're the bait." She makes a rough noise in the back of her throat. "Don't worry. I won't press you to tell me who. And I don't blame you for hiding out. Carl's brilliant, but he's a bit of a prick."

"It's the brilliant part I signed on for," I say, and she barks out a laugh.

The truth is that she's right about me being the bait. "Wear a cocktail dress," Carl had said. "Something flirty."

Seriously? I mean, *Seriously?*

I should have told him to wear his own damn cocktail dress. But I didn't. Because I want this job. I fought to get this job. Carl's company, C-Squared Technologies, successfully launched three web-based products in the last eighteen months. That track record had caught the industry's eye, and Carl had been hailed as a man to watch.

More important from my perspective, that meant he was a man to learn from, and I'd prepared for the job interview with an intensity bordering on obsession. Landing the position had been a huge coup for me. So what if he wanted me to wear something flirty? It was a small price to pay.

Shit.

"I need to get back to being the bait," I say.

"Oh, hell. Now I've gone and made you feel either guilty or self-conscious. Don't be. Let them get liquored up in there first. You catch more flies with alcohol anyway. Trust me. I know."

She's holding a pack of cigarettes, and now she taps one out, then extends the pack to me. I shake my head. I love the smell of tobacco—it reminds me of my grandfather—but actually inhaling the smoke does nothing for me.

"I'm too old and set in my ways to quit," she says. "But God forbid I smoke in my own damn house. I swear, the mob would burn me in effigy. You're not going to start lecturing me on the dangers of secondhand smoke, are you?"

"No," I promise.

"Then how about a light?"

I hold up the itty-bitty purse. "One lipstick, a credit card, my driver's license, and my phone."

"No condom?"

"I didn't think it was that kind of party," I say dryly.

"I knew I liked you." She glances around the balcony. "What the hell kind of party am I throwing if I don't even have one goddamn candle on one goddamn table? Well, fuck it." She puts the unlit cigarette to her mouth and inhales, her eyes closed and her expression rapturous. I can't help but like her. She wears hardly any makeup, in stark contrast to all the other women here tonight, myself included, and her dress is more of a caftan, the batik pattern as interesting as the woman herself.

She's what my mother would call a brassy broad—

loud, large, opinionated, and self-confident. My mother would hate her. I think she's awesome.

She drops the unlit cigarette onto the tile and grinds it with the toe of her shoe. Then she signals to one of the catering staff, a girl dressed all in black and carrying a tray of champagne glasses.

The girl fumbles for a minute with the sliding door that opens onto the balcony, and I imagine those flutes tumbling off, breaking against the hard tile, the scattered shards glittering like a wash of diamonds.

I picture myself bending to snatch up a broken stem. I see the raw edge cutting into the soft flesh at the base of my thumb as I squeeze. I watch myself clutching it tighter, drawing strength from the pain, the way some people might try to extract luck from a rabbit's foot.

The fantasy blurs with memory, jarring me with its potency. It's fast and powerful, and a little disturbing because I haven't needed the pain in a long time, and I don't understand why I'm thinking about it now, when I feel steady and in control.

I am fine, I think. *I am fine, I am fine, I am fine.*

"Take one, honey," Evelyn says easily, holding a flute out to me.

I hesitate, searching her face for signs that my mask has slipped and she's caught a glimpse of my rawness. But her face is clear and genial.

"No, don't you argue," she adds, misinterpreting my hesitation. "I bought a dozen cases and I hate to see good alcohol go to waste. Hell no," she adds when the girl tries to hand her a flute. "I hate the stuff. Get me a vodka. Straight up. Chilled. Four olives. Hurry up, now. Do you want me to dry up like a leaf and float away?"

The girl shakes her head, looking a bit like a twitchy, frightened rabbit. Possibly one that had sacrificed his foot for someone else's good luck.

Evelyn's attention returns to me. "So how do you like LA? What have you seen? Where have you been? Have you bought a map of the stars yet? Dear God, tell me you're not getting sucked into all that tourist bullshit."

"Mostly I've seen miles of freeway and the inside of my apartment."

"Well, that's just sad. Makes me even more glad

that Carl dragged your skinny ass all the way out here tonight."

I've put on fifteen welcome pounds since the years when my mother monitored every tiny thing that went in my mouth, and while I'm perfectly happy with my size-eight ass, I wouldn't describe it as skinny. I know Evelyn means it as a compliment, though, and so I smile. "I'm glad he brought me, too. The paintings really are amazing."

"Now don't do that—don't you go sliding into the polite-conversation routine. No, no," she says before I can protest. "I'm sure you mean it. Hell, the paintings are wonderful. But you're getting the flat-eyed look of a girl on her best behavior, and we can't have that. Not when I was getting to know the real you."

"Sorry," I say. "I swear I'm not fading away on you."

Because I genuinely like her, I don't tell her that she's wrong—she hasn't met the real Nikki Fairchild. She's met Social Nikki who, much like Malibu Barbie, comes with a complete set of accessories. In my case, it's not a bikini and a convertible.

Instead, I have the *Elizabeth Fairchild Guide for Social Gatherings*.

My mother's big on rules. She claims it's her Southern upbringing. In my weaker moments, I agree. Mostly, I just think she's a controlling bitch. Since the first time she took me for tea at the Mansion at Turtle Creek in Dallas at age three, I have had the rules drilled into my head. How to walk, how to talk, how to dress. What to eat, how much to drink, what kinds of jokes to tell.

I have it all down, every trick, every nuance, and I wear my practiced pageant smile like armor against the world. The result being that I don't think I could truly be myself at a party even if my life depended on it.

This, however, is not something Evelyn needs to know.

"Where exactly are you living?" she asks.

"Studio City. I'm sharing a condo with my best friend from high school."

"Straight down the 101 for work and then back home again. No wonder you've only seen concrete.

Didn't anyone tell you that you should have taken an apartment on the Westside?"

"Too pricey to go it alone," I admit, and I can tell that my admission surprises her. When I make the effort—like when I'm Social Nikki—I can't help but look like I come from money. Probably because I do. Come from it, that is. But that doesn't mean I brought it with me.

"How old are you?"

"Twenty-four."

Evelyn nods sagely, as if my age reveals some secret about me. "You'll be wanting a place of your own soon enough. You call me when you do and we'll find you someplace with a view. Not as good as this one, of course, but we can manage something better than a freeway on-ramp."

"It's not that bad, I promise."

"Of course it's not," she says in a tone that says the exact opposite. "As for views," she continues, gesturing toward the now-dark ocean and the sky that's starting to bloom with stars, "you're welcome to come back anytime and share mine."

"I might take you up on that," I admit. "I'd love to

bring a decent camera back here and take a shot or two."

"It's an open invitation. I'll provide the wine and you can provide the entertainment. A young woman loose in the city. Will it be a drama? A rom-com? Not a tragedy, I hope. I love a good cry as much as the next woman, but I like you. You need a happy ending."

I tense, but Evelyn doesn't know she's hit a nerve. That's why I moved to LA, after all. New life. New story. New Nikki.

I ramp up the Social Nikki smile and lift my champagne flute. "To happy endings. And to this amazing party. I think I've kept you from it long enough."

"Bullshit," she says. "I'm the one monopolizing you, and we both know it."

We slip back inside, the buzz of alcohol-fueled conversation replacing the soft calm of the ocean.

"The truth is, I'm a terrible hostess. I do what I want, talk to whoever I want, and if my guests feel slighted they can damn well deal with it."

I gape. I can almost hear my mother's cries of horror all the way from Dallas.

"Besides," she continues, "this party isn't supposed to be about me. I put together this little shindig to introduce Blaine and his art to the community. He's the one who should be doing the mingling, not me. I may be fucking him, but I'm not going to baby him."

Evelyn has completely destroyed my image of how a hostess for the not-to-be-missed social event of the weekend is supposed to behave, and I think I'm a little in love with her for that.

"I haven't met Blaine yet. That's him, right?" I point to a tall reed of a man. He is bald, but sports a red goatee. I'm pretty sure it's not his natural color. A small crowd hums around him, like bees drawing nectar from a flower. His outfit is certainly as bright as one.

"That's my little center of attention, all right," Evelyn says. "The man of the hour. Talented, isn't he?" Her hand sweeps out to indicate her massive living room. Every wall is covered with paintings. Except for a few benches, whatever furniture was once in the room has been removed and replaced with easels on which more paintings stand.

I suppose technically they are portraits. The models are nudes, but these aren't like anything you would see in a classical art book. There's something edgy about them. Something provocative and raw. I can tell that they are expertly conceived and carried out, and yet they disturb me, as if they reveal more about the person viewing the portrait than about the painter or the model.

As far as I can tell, I'm the only one with that reaction. Certainly the crowd around Blaine is glowing. I can hear the gushing praise from here.

"I picked a winner with that one," Evelyn says. "But let's see. Who do you want to meet? Rip Carrington and Lyle Tarpin? Those two are guaranteed drama, that's for damn sure, and your roommate will be jealous as hell if you chat them up."

"She will?"

Evelyn's brows arch up. "Rip and Lyle? They've been feuding for weeks." She narrows her eyes at me. "The fiasco about the new season of their sitcom? It's all over the Internet? You really don't know them?"

"Sorry," I say, feeling the need to apologize. "My school schedule was pretty intense. And I'm sure you can imagine what working for Carl is like."

Speaking of ...

I glance around, but I don't see my boss anywhere.

"That is one serious gap in your education," Evelyn says. "Culture—and yes, pop culture counts—is just as important as—what did you say you studied?"

"I don't think I mentioned it. But I have a double major in electrical engineering and computer science."

"So you've got brains and beauty. See? That's something else we have in common. Gotta say, though, with an education like that, I don't see why you signed up to be Carl's secretary."

I laugh. "I'm not, I swear. Carl was looking for someone with tech experience to work with him on the business side of things, and I was looking for a job where I could learn the business side. Get my feet wet. I think he was a little hesitant to hire me at first—my skills definitely lean toward tech—but I convinced him I'm a fast learner."

She peers at me. "I smell ambition."

I lift a shoulder in a casual shrug. "It's Los Angeles. Isn't that what this town is all about?"

"Ha! Carl's lucky he's got you. It'll be interesting to see how long he keeps you. But let's see … who here would intrigue you …?"

She casts about the room, finally pointing to a fifty-something man holding court in a corner. "That's Charles Maynard," she says. "I've known Charlie for years. Intimidating as hell until you get to know him. But it's worth it. His clients are either celebrities with name recognition or power brokers with more money than God. Either way, he's got all the best stories."

"He's a lawyer?"

"With Bender, Twain & McGuire. Very prestigious firm."

"I know," I say, happy to show that I'm not entirely ignorant, despite not knowing Rip or Lyle. "One of my closest friends works for the firm. He started here but he's in their New York office now."

"Well, come on, then, Texas. I'll introduce you." We take one step in that direction, but then Evelyn stops me. Maynard has pulled out his phone, and is shouting instructions at someone. I catch a few well-placed curses and eye Evelyn sideways. She looks unconcerned "He's a pussycat at heart. Trust me, I've worked with him before. Back in my agenting days, we put together more celebrity biopic deals for our clients than I can count. And we fought to keep a few tell-alls off the screen, too." She shakes her head, as if reliving those glory days, then pats my arm. "Still, we'll wait 'til he calms down a bit. In the meantime, though ..."

She trails off, and the corners of her mouth turn down in a frown as she scans the room again. "I don't think he's here yet, but—oh! Yes! Now *there's* someone you should meet. And if you want to talk views, the house he's building has one that makes my view look like, well, like yours." She points toward the entrance hall, but all I see are bobbing heads and haute couture. "He hardly ever accepts invitations, but we go way back," she says.

I still can't see who she's talking about, but then the crowd parts and I see the man in profile. Goose bumps rise on my arms, but I'm not cold. In fact, I'm suddenly very, very warm.

He's tall and so handsome that the word is almost an insult. But it's more than that. It's not his looks, it's his *presence*. He commands the room simply by being in it, and I realize that Evelyn and I aren't the only ones looking at him. The entire crowd has noticed his arrival. He must feel the weight of all those eyes, and yet the attention doesn't faze him at all. He smiles at the girl with the champagne, takes a glass, and begins to chat casually with a woman who approaches him, a simpering smile stretched across her face.

"Damn that girl," Evelyn says. "She never did bring me my vodka."

But I barely hear her. "Damien Stark," I say. My voice surprises me. It's little more than breath.

Evelyn's brows rise so high I notice the movement in my peripheral vision. "Well, how about that?" she says knowingly. "Looks like I guessed right."

"You did," I admit. "Mr. Stark is just the man I want to see."

I hope you enjoyed the excerpt! Grab your own copy of Release Me … or any of the books in the series now!

The Original Trilogy

Release Me

Claim Me

Complete Me

And Beyond...

Anchor Me

Lost With Me

Some rave reviews for J. Kenner's sizzling romances...

I just get sucked into these books and can not get enough of this series. They are so well written and as satisfying as each book is they leave you greedy for more. — Goodreads reviewer on *Wicked Torture*

A sizzling, intoxicating, sexy read!!!! J. Kenner had me devouring Wicked Dirty, the second installment of *Stark World Series* in one sitting. I loved everything about this book from the opening pages to the raw and vulnerable characters. With her sophisticated prose, Kenner created a love story that had the perfect blend of lust, passion, sexual tension, raw emotions and love. - Michelle, Four Chicks Flipping Pages

Wicked Dirty CLAIMED and CONSUMED every ounce of me from the very first page. Mind racing. Pulse pounding. Breaths bated. Feels flowing. Eyes wide in anticipation. Heart beating out of my chest. I felt the current of *Wicked Dirty* flow through me. I was DRUNK on this book that was my fine whiskey, so smooth and spectacular, and could not get enough of this *Wicked Dirty* drink. - Karen Bookalicious Babes Blog

"Sinfully sexy and full of heart. Kenner shines in this second chance, slow burn of a romance. Wicked Grind is the perfect book to kick off your summer."- *K. Bromberg, New York Times bestselling author (on Wicked Grind)*

"J. Kenner never disappoints~her books just get better and better." - *Mom's Guilty Pleasure (on Wicked Grind)*

"I don't think J. Kenner could write a bad story if she tried. ... Wicked Grind is a great beginning to what I'm positive will be a very successful series. ... The line forms here." *iScream Books (On Wicked Grind)*

"Scorching, sweet, and soul-searing, *Anchor Me* is the ultimate love story that stands the test of time and tribulation. THE TRUEST LOVE!" *Bookalicious Babes Blog (on Anchor Me)*

"J. Kenner has brought this couple to life and the character connection that I have to these two holds no bounds and that is testament to J.

Kenner's writing ability." *The Romance Cover (on Anchor Me)*

"J. Kenner writes an emotional and personal story line. ... The premise will captivate your imagination; the characters will break your heart; the romance continues to push the envelope." *The Reading Café (on Anchor Me)*

"Kenner may very well have cornered the market on sinfully attractive, dominant antiheroes and the women who swoon for them . . ." *Romantic Times*

"*Wanted* is another J. Kenner masterpiece . . . This was an intriguing look at self-discovery and forbidden love all wrapped into a neat little action-suspense package. There was plenty of sexual tension and eventually action. Evan was hot, hot, hot! Together, they were combustible. But can we expect anything less from J. Kenner?" *Reading Haven*

"*Wanted* by J. Kenner is the whole package! A toe-curling smokin' hot read, full of incredible characters and a brilliant storyline that you won't be able to get enough of. I can't wait for the next book in this series . . . I'm hooked!" *Flirty & Dirty Book Blog*

"J. Kenner's evocative writing thrillingly captures the power of physical attraction, the pull of longing, the universe-altering effect one person can have on another. . . . *Claim Me* has the emotional depth to back up the sex . . . Every scene is infused with both erotic tension, and the tension of wondering what lies beneath Damien's veneer – and how and when it will be revealed." *Heroes and Heartbreakers*

"*Claim Me* by J. Kenner is an erotic, sexy and exciting ride. The story between Damien and Nikki is amazing and written beautifully. The intimate and detailed sex scenes will leave you fanning yourself to cool down. With the writing style of Ms. Kenner you almost feel like you are there in the story riding along the emotional rollercoaster with Damien and Nikki." *Fresh Fiction*

"PERFECT for fans of *Fifty Shades of Grey* and *Bared to You*. *Release Me* is a powerful and erotic romance novel that is sure to make adult romance readers sweat, sigh and swoon." *Reading, Eating & Dreaming Blog*

"I will admit, I am in the 'I loved *Fifty Shades*' camp,

but after reading *Release Me*, Mr. Grey only scratches the surface compared to Damien Stark." *Cocktails and Books Blog*

"It is not often when a book is so amazingly well-written that I find it hard to even begin to accurately describe it . . . I recommend this book to everyone who is interested in a passionate love story." *Romancebookworm's Reviews*

"The story is one that will rank up with the *Fifty Shades* and Cross Fire trilogies." *Incubus Publishing Blog*

"The plot is complex, the characters engaging, and J. Kenner's passionate writing brings it all perfectly together." *Harlequin Junkie*

Also by J. Kenner

The Stark Saga Novels:

Only his passion could set her free…

Meet Damien Stark

The Original Trilogy

Release Me

Claim Me

Complete Me

And Beyond…

Anchor Me

Lost With Me

Stark Ever After

(Stark Saga novellas):

Happily ever after is just the beginning.

The passion between Damien & Nikki continues.

Take Me

Have Me

Play My Game

Seduce Me

Unwrap Me

Deepest Kiss

Entice Me

Hold Me

Please Me

The Steele Books / Stark International:

He was the only man who made her feel alive.

Say My Name

On My Knees

Under My Skin

Take My Dare (includes short story Steal My Heart)

Stark International Novellas:

Meet Jamie & Ryan-so hot it sizzles.

Tame Me

Tempt Me

S.I.N. Trilogy:

It was wrong for them to be together…

…but harder to stay apart.

Dirtiest Secret

Hottest Mess

Sweetest Taboo

Stand alone novels:

Most Wanted:

Three powerful, dangerous men.

Three sensual, seductive women.

Wanted

Heated

Ignited

Wicked Nights (Stark World):

Sometimes it feels so damn good to be bad.

Wicked Grind

Wicked Dirty

Wicked Torture

Man of the Month

Who's your man of the month …?

Down On Me

Hold On Tight

Need You Now

Start Me Up

Get It On

In Your Eyes

Turn Me On

Shake It Up

All Night Long

In Too Deep

Light My Fire

Walk The Line

Bar Bites: A Man of the Month Cookbook(by J. Kenner & Suzanne M. Johnson)

Additional Titles

Wild Thing

One Night (A Stark World short story in the Second Chances anthology)

Also by Julie Kenner

The Protector (Superhero) Series:

The Cat's Fancy (prequel)

Aphrodite's Kiss

Aphrodite's Passion

Aphrodite's Secret

Aphrodite's Flame

Aphrodite's Embrace (novella)

Aphrodite's Delight (novella – free download)

Demon Hunting Soccer Mom Series:

Carpe Demon

California Demon

Demons Are Forever

Deja Demon

The Demon You Know (short story)

Demon Ex Machina

Pax Demonica

Day of the Demon

About the Author

J. Kenner (aka Julie Kenner) is the *New York Times*, *USA Today*, *Publishers Weekly*, *Wall Street Journal* and #1 International bestselling author of over one hundred novels, novellas and short stories in a variety of genres.

JK has been praised by *Publishers Weekly* as an author with a "flair for dialogue and eccentric characterizations" and by *RT Bookclub* for having "cornered the market on sinfully attractive, dominant antiheroes and the women who swoon for them." A six-time finalist for Romance Writers of America's prestigious RITA award, JK took home the first RITA trophy awarded in the category of erotic romance in 2014 for her novel, *Claim Me* (book 2 of her Stark Trilogy).

In her previous career as an attorney, JK worked as a lawyer in Southern California and Texas. She currently lives in Central Texas, with her husband, two daughters, and two rather spastic cats.

More ways to connect:
www.jkenner.com
Text JKenner to 21000 for JK's text alerts.

facebook.com/jkennerbooks

twitter.com/juliekenner

Made in the USA
Columbia, SC
14 June 2018